READ ALL OF CHEESIE'S ADVENTURES!

CHEESIE MACK

IS RUNNING LIKE CRAZY!

STEVE COTLER

Illustrated by Douglas Holgate

random house 🏠 new york

Text copyright © 2013 by Stephen L. Cotler
Jacket art and interior illustrations copyright © 2013 by Douglas Holgate

Visit us on the Web! randomhouse.com/kids

Educators and librarians, for a variety of teaching tools,
visit us at RHTeachersLibrarians.com

Visit Cheesie at CheesieMack.com!

Library of Congress Cataloging-in-Publication Data
Cotler, Stephen L.
Cheesie Mack is running like crazy! / Steve Cotler ; illustrated by Douglas Holgate. — 1st ed.
p. cm.
Summary: Sixth-grader Ronald "Cheesie" Mack finds the best way to earn points against his older sister is to become popular, and decides to join the cross-country team, help his best friend run for class president, and ignore her attempts to embarrass him.
ISBN 978-0-307-97713-7 (trade) — ISBN 978-0-307-97714-4 (lib. bdg.) —
ISBN 978-0-307-97715-1 (ebook) — ISBN 978-0-307-97716-8 (pbk.)
[1. Brothers and sisters—Fiction. 2. Elections—Fiction. 3. Best friends—Fiction.
4. Friendship—Fiction. 5. Track and field—Fiction. 6. Middle schools—Fiction.
7. Schools—Fiction.] I. Holgate, Douglas, ill. II. Title.
PZ7.C82862Chs 2013 [Fic]—dc23 2012017978

Printed in the United States of America

10 9 8 7 6 5 4 3 2 1

First Edition

For Lanny and Doug . . . my brothers,
creative partners, and BFFs. And for Mr. C,
my middle school coach, who saw my passion
and put me on the basketball team in spite
of short stature and total lack of talent.

Contents

Chapter 22

Preview of Coming Attractions

This book contains the absolutely true story of my third adventure, and you probably think you're at the beginning of that story.

Well, you're not!

This is actually the last chapter.

Sort of.

What I mean is, I wrote this chapter last.

I'm Ronald Mack, but everyone calls me Cheesie. If you can't guess why, then you probably don't like a certain kind of pasta glopped all over with a certain kind of dairy product.

This chapter is like the previews of coming attractions you watch before the real movie starts, and if you're like me, you really enjoy those previews. So pretend you're in the theater with a bag of popcorn and a box of candy, the room is dark, and on the screen are the words: *Cheesie Mack Is Running Like Crazy!*

If that title makes you guess there'll be lots of running in my movie, you'd be right.

But there's lots of other stuff, too:

1. The most evil teenager in the universe.
2. Courageous knights who collide in bone-breaking jousts.
3. Microscopic face bugs.
4. A dancing squid.
5. The weirdest election in the history of the sixth grade.

That's what's coming. That's my preview.

So go ahead. Finish this chapter and turn the page. That's when the *Cheesie Mack Is Running Like Crazy!* story will start playing like a movie in your own mind.

It begins at the beginning of middle school. If you like it or don't or can't make up your mind, please go to my website and tell me.

Signed:

Ronald "Cheesie" Mack

Ronald "Cheesie" Mack (age 11 years and 3 months)

CheesieMack.com

Chapter 1

Doofus, Dweeb, and Dork-Boy

Today was my first day at Robert Louis Stevenson Middle School. Everyone calls it RLS. But before I tell you about my new school (I'm in sixth grade), here are a few things you should know about me and my life:

1. Georgie Sinkoff is my best friend. Our houses are next to each other but not on the same street. (If you read either of my previous books, you know why.) He lives with his father.

2. I live with my mother, father, grandfather, and sister. My sister's name is June, but I call her Goon. She is an eighth grader at

RLS. She is despicable, a word that describes someone who is evil, nasty, mean, selfish, and _____. (There are lots of other words that describe sisters like Goon. Pick one. You can write it in the blank . . . *unless this is a library book!*)

3. Goon and I have been fighting and arguing

 for as long as I have been alive. But since the beginning of fourth grade, I have been keeping a private tally of who's winning. I call it the Point Battle. No one else knows about it. (The rules I use for the Point Battle are in my first two books and on my website. Believe me, they're complicated, but fair.) At the end of *Cool in a Duel*, my second adventure, I was leading by just one point: 669–668. That was when camp ended. Unfortunately, for the rest of the summer Goon tortured and teased me and mostly got away with it. She's ahead again.

The Point Battle score as of the beginning of school was 682–673.

4. Georgie is big. At Rocky Neck Elementary  School, he was the way biggest fifth grader. At RLS, he will be the second-tallest sixth grader. Ms. Dinnington, the school nurse (who is his father's girlfriend, more on that later), told Georgie a girl from Iceland moved here over the summer and she is almost an inch taller. Georgie is strong, athletic, and not afraid of anyone. He has greenish-brown eyes, reddish-brown hair, glasses with bright red frames, and braces.

5. I am not so big. I was the shortest in fourth grade, second shortest in fifth, and in sixth grade, I'm guessing I'll be about 20 percent from the bottom. I do not have braces, but Mom says I may get them later this year. I have brown hair, brown eyes, and both my second toes are longer than my big toes.

6. I have lived all my life in Gloucester, a small town on the Atlantic Ocean in eastern Massachusetts. (Do not say GLOUW-sess-ter, even though that's what it looks like. It's GLAH-stir, but most people in this part of Massachusetts pronounce it GLAH-stah because there's a real shortage of *r*'s around here. Maybe it should be spelled Glosta.) I once looked at Gloucester in a satellite image on my computer and zoomed in until I could actually see one of my father's limousines parked in front of our house. (He owns a company that drives people around.) If I'd known the satellite was going to take that picture, I would've spray-painted "Cheesie Lives Here" on my roof. My dad has a great sense of humor. He would've let me do it. How cool would that be?!

That's enough background stuff. My sixth-grade adventure starts now.

* * *

I bounced out of bed with a grin on my face. It was the first day of school, and I had been dreaming about being the only kid with an anti-gravity bicycle.

I yawned hugely and walked down the hall to the bathroom. As usual, Goon was locked inside, hogging it.

"Hurry up!" I shouted, pounding on the door.

"Get lost!" she yelled back.

I wasn't in a hurry, so I smacked the door four more times, then went back to my room to put the last few items into my SuperBinder. A SuperBinder is required for every kid who starts sixth grade at Stevenson Middle School. You're allowed to decorate the outside of your SuperBinder any way you want, but I hadn't decided yet, so mine was blank. Here's what has to be in it:

1. The RLS school rule book.
2. Your class schedule.
3. The homework website information sheet.
4. Lots of three-hole lined paper.
5. Subject dividers.
6. A pencil pouch containing five sharpened

pencils, an eraser, a ruler, and lots of
other stuff.

7. A chunk of dry ice.

8. About ten other items.

I'm kidding about the dry ice. I just wanted to see if you're the kind of reader who gets bored with lists and skips to the end.

Dry ice is weird. It's not ice at all. It's actually frozen carbon dioxide, and if you put a chunk in water, it creates bubbles of white water vapor and CO_2. Lots of Halloween displays use dry ice because the bubbles look sort of spooky.

"You can have the bathroom, Runto!" Goon shouted from the hallway. I closed my SuperBinder and ran. Now I was in a hurry—I guess because I'd been thinking about bubbling water, if you get what I mean.

Bathroom, get dressed, breakfast . . . just like every kid does. I was so focused on getting ready, I didn't keep track of the enemy. Big mistake! By the time I went back upstairs to grab my school stuff, Goon had "decorated" my SuperBinder in a hideous way, which I will describe in a moment.

I didn't have time to hide what she'd done, so I stashed the binder in my backpack and ran downstairs. Granpa looked up from his coffee and newspaper.

"Good luck at school, kiddo," he said. "Go, Panthers!"

I zoomed by him and yelled back, "Pirates, not Panthers!" (The RLS school mascot is a fighting pirate.)

Granpa gave me a squinty-evil-eye, which let me know he was just kidding (and made him look like a fighting pirate!). The squinty-evil-eye is what Granpa, Dad, and I do when we're teasing each other. It's a Mack Family Tradition.

Seconds later I was outside and pedaling my bike. Georgie was waiting on his bike at the end of my block. "First day race?" he challenged, and we took off!

I won. I almost always do. Bike riding is the one sport where I am totally better than Georgie.

By the time we got inside the school, I had completely forgotten what Goon had done to my

SuperBinder. The corridors were hubbubbing with kids talking, laughing, and high-fiving.

New schools can be really confusing. It took me a few minutes of wandering to find my locker. Then I struggled to work the combination. It didn't help that Georgie was leaning next to me repeating over and over in a singsong voice, "Middle school is totally cool. Middle school is totally cool."

When I messed up my locker combination for the third time (Georgie's fault!), I spun around and pushed him. That's when I saw Goon and her new boyfriend, Drew Teague, staring at me from across the hall.

Goon used to like Kevin Welch (the older brother of Alex Welch, who is in my grade). But when Kevin and I became sort-of friends (if you read *Cool in a Duel*, you know how that happened), Goon called him a traitor and dumped him. About a minute later she texted Drew and told him he could be her new boyfriend.

I finally got my locker open and stashed my lunch, but just as I closed it, Drew swooped in, grabbed my backpack off the floor, and passed it to Goon. I snatched it back, but not before Goon had pulled my SuperBinder out.

"Look, everybody!" Goon shouted. "My twerpy brother has done an amazing job on his SuperBinder!"

I leaped at her, but she zigzagged down the hallway, holding the binder up for everyone to see what she'd scribbled: DOOFUS in red marker (big!) on one side, DWEEB (bigger!) on the other, and DORK-BOY (biggest!!!) down the spine.

Kids looked at me.

Kids pointed at me.

Goon was laughing so hard she had to stop and bend over.

I was totally humiliated.

I grabbed my SuperBinder and hurried back to my locker. I tried to cover up her graffiti insults, but I didn't have enough arms.

Sixth grade was less than five minutes old, and Goon had already beaten me for eight points, increasing her lead in the Point Battle to seventeen (690–673).

Here's how I calculated my loss. Goon had embarrassed me when other people were around—four points—which doubled to eight because my red face proved it was an excellent insult. Darn.

Okay. So she had won the first round at RLS, but the Point Battle was far from over. An eighth grader versus a sixth grader would not normally be a fair fight. But this was the Point Battle—Goon versus Cheesie Mack—and Cheesie Mack was determined to win.

AMAZING
CHEESEMAN
VS.
HIDEOUS
GOON

Chapter 2

June Mack's Little Brother

"Looks like you're going to be in a Sister War all year," Georgie said as we started down the corridor toward room 113. Then he took a deep breath and held it all the way down the hall. Georgie says it strengthens your lungs and makes you a better athlete. I think he just likes holding his breath.

Room 113 was our homeroom. It was also where we had Core—language arts and social studies—for the first two periods every day. When we walked in, lots of kids were chattering. All but two seats were taken, so it was easy to find the desks that had our names on them. I was in the second row near the middle.

Georgie's desk was all the way in the back corner. As he walked to it, he let out his air in a big blast . . . *POOF!* It was so loud, it made lots of kids look up from their talking. Georgie just grinned at them.

I slid into my chair and opened my SuperBinder, carefully placing it covers-down on my desk so no one could see what Goon had done to it. Then I looked around. Of the twenty-four kids in the room (four rows of desks, with six desks in each row), seven were from my fifth-grade class at Rocky Neck Elementary, including Glenn Philips, Lana Shen, Georgie, and me.

You probably remember Glenn from my first book. He is smaller than I am and super smart. Lana is also smaller than I am, but I don't know if she's smarter. She's okay, I guess, but she always wants to talk to me.

I glanced at her. She was staring at me. When she saw me looking over, she gave me a huge wave. My return wave was smaller.

Sitting to my left was a super-tall girl with light hair and blue eyes. I glanced at her name card. If you guessed that she was the girl from Iceland, you're right. She had an odd name: Oddny Thorsdottir.

I flipped through my SuperBinder and looked at my class schedule.

Here it is:

Period	Subject	Room	Teacher
1	Core—lang arts/soc stud	113	Mrs. Wikowitz
2	Core		
3	Science	220	Mr. Amato
4	Math	106	Ms. Hammerbord
LUNCH			
5	(M) Music	A-3	Mr. Noa
5	(T, Th) Spanish	229	Mrs. Lunares
5	(W) Art	230	Ms. Charles
5	(F) Technology	102	Ms. Waring
6	Physical Education	Gym	Coach Tunavelov

I looked up at the wall clock. In exactly one minute, sixth grade would start and I'd officially be a middle schooler.

Just then a tall woman walked into the room.

She was dressed entirely in black. All kid chatter stopped immediately. Without a word, the teacher turned her back to the class and began writing on the whiteboard: *Mrs. Wikowitz*. Then she turned around and said, "Good morning, students. Please open your SuperBinders to the Stevenson Middle School rule book."

My mother says I shouldn't trust first impressions. "They are just hints, nothing more," she says.

My father doesn't agree. He says, "First meetings can tell a lot about a person."

Granpa, as usual, has a crazy opinion. He says, "You let me eyeball anyone just once and I'll tell you her favorite holiday, whether she likes chili on hot dogs, and if she can ride a unicycle."

My first impressions of Mrs. Wikowitz were:

1. She wasn't smiling, so she was unfriendly.

2. She stood perfectly straight and didn't

Not smiling (unfriendly)

Stands perfectly straight

fidget even the tiniest bit, so she expected our full attention.

3. She was eyeing everyone, so she wouldn't tolerate any monkey business.

I admit my logic was weak, but it turned out I was right on all three points.

"I would like each of you to read one of the school rules aloud," Mrs. Wikowitz said. She pointed at Lana, who sat in the front row, all the way on the right. "You may begin."

Seven kids read, and then Oddny. She read perfectly, but with an accent that was sort of musical. I was staring at her and thinking that I had never met anyone from Iceland before, and that I had learned somewhere that they are all descended from Vikings. I forgot it was my turn.

Mrs. Wikowitz said, "Ronald Mack? Number nine, please."

I jerked my eyes back to the school rule book and read:

Descendants?!

"Upon receiving a third tardy notice, students will not be admitted to class, but must instead go to the principal's office and obtain a re-admit."

The kid on my right, a boy I'd never met—Eddie Chapple, according to his name card—was next. He was supposed to read:

"A fourth tardy will result in a one-day suspension from school and require a student/parent meeting with the principal."

Instead he read:

"A forced party will insult in a one-way suspicion of skill and require a prudent parrot beaten by the prince of pull."

Then he looked up and grinned.

Lots of kids, me included, laughed.

"Please read that again, Edward," Mrs. Wikowitz said firmly but without raising her voice.

Eddie did . . . this time the right way. When he finished, I expected Mrs. Wikowitz to call on the next student, but she just stared at Eddie, then picked up a pencil, took a small blue pad of paper out of her desk drawer, and wrote. It took her almost a half minute to finish the note. The whole time, no one made a sound.

Finally she tore the note off the pad and held it at arm's length.

"Ronald Mack, please stand."

I stood instantly, completely surprised—what had I done?—and knocked my SuperBinder to the floor. It flipped over, and lots of kids saw *Doofus, Dweeb, and Dork-Boy*. Some of them giggled. I was kind of embarrassed, and so, even though Goon wasn't there, I had to award her another four points. The score was 694–673. Darn.

"Ronald," Mrs. Wikowitz said, "would you please take this note and accompany Edward to the principal's office? You are to see that he arrives there without delay. No bathroom stops. No dawdling. No conversation. Please give this note to the secretary, and after Edward has discussed his behavior with Mr. Stotts, you both shall return to this room in the same fashion. Do you understand?"

I put my SuperBinder back on my desk (with the covers facedown!), said, "Yes, ma'am," and walked to her desk.

She handed me the blue slip. "Edward, please go with Ronald."

Eddie stood, strode to the door, and pushed it open. I scooted through just before it closed.

In the hallway, Eddie looked back at room 113 and muttered something I am not allowed to write. Then he started walking fast. I followed him, realizing I had no idea where the principal's office was.

"Where're you going?" I asked.

"Mr. Stotts's office, like the teacher said." He didn't even look at me. He just kept striding along. I had to sort of trot to keep up.

The best word to describe Eddie Chapple is *jagged*. He is tall and skinny, and when he moves it looks like he has lots of elbows and knees. He has a pointy nose and a pointy chin and pointy eyebrows. His hair is cut and gelled with spikes. He would stand out in any crowd of kids. But this morning in class Eddie Chapple had made himself stand out even more.

At the end of the hall, I saw an OFFICE sign with an arrow pointing down another corridor. Eddie stopped underneath the sign, snatched the note out of my hand, and crumpled it into a really tight ball.

"Watch this." He turned, raised his hands, then launched a long basketball-style jump shot across the hallway at a not-so-big opening of a recycling bin. The paper ball dropped right through! Even Georgie couldn't have done that.

"Great shot," I said.

"Basketball's my best sport," Eddie replied with an almost-smile. "And no matter what Mrs. Wicked Witch thinks, I have just proved I am a good citizen by recycling her note. What's yours?"

At first I didn't know what he was asking, then I said, "Baseball."

We walked down the hall to the school office, which was like the office at any other school. You can probably guess what it looked like.

The office secretary was on the phone. She gave Eddie a huge smile and a hold-on-a-minute wave. Her super-thick glasses made her eyes look gigantic. The nameplate on her desk said MRS. COLLINS.

"Hello again, Eddie," she said after she hung up. Then she huge-smiled me. "Which of you has the blue slip?"

Eddie was already taking a seat and didn't look like he was going to answer, so I said, "Um, I do. I mean, I did. I, uh . . . I'll go get it."

The halls were deserted, so I half ran to the recy-cling bin, wondering if I was going to get in trouble for running. I was peering into the opening of the bin when a very short, very round man walked by.

"Lose something?" he asked, slowing but not stopping.

"I just found it," I replied, holding up the little wad of blue paper.

"Blue slip? Too bad for you," Mr. Amato said.

(How did I know the very short, very round teacher's name? Actually, at that moment, I didn't. I'm just sticking it in here because you'll meet him soon!)

He called out, "See you in third period . . . and no running," as I speed-walked back to the office. I unwadded the blue slip and handed it to the secretary. Then I sat down next to Eddie. And we waited.

And waited.

And waited.

It was boring, so I read the papers thumbtacked to the bulletin board on the opposite wall of the office. Most of it was stuff like bus schedules and lunch menus. But one paper caught my eye.

I'd heard a lot about student government because Goon is the eighth-grade vice president. They'd had their election at the end of last year when they were seventh graders. She brags about being VP a lot. She

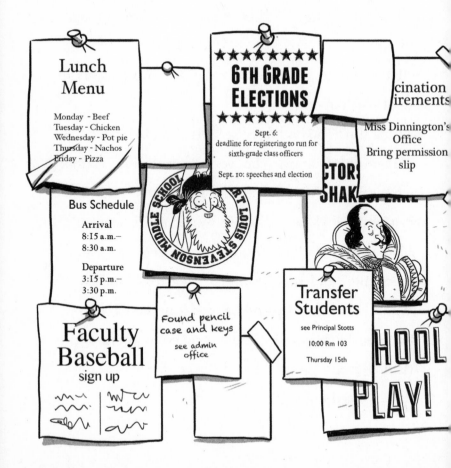

Lunch
Menu

Monday - Beef
Tuesday - Chicken
Wednesday - Pot pie
Thursday - Nachos
Friday - Pizza

★★★★★★★★★★
6TH GRADE ELECTIONS
★★★★★★★★★★

Sept. 6:
deadline for registering to run for
sixth-grade class officers

Sept. 10: speeches and election

cination
irements

Miss Dinnington's
Office
Bring permission
slip

Bus Schedule

Arrival
8:15 a.m.–
8:30 a.m.

Departure
3:15 p.m.–
3:30 p.m.

ROBERT LOUIS STEVENSON MIDDLE SCHOOL

TORS
SHAKESPEARE

Faculty
Baseball
sign up

Found pencil
case and keys

see admin
office

Transfer
Students

see Principal Stotts

10:00 Rm 103

Thursday 15th

HOOL
PLAY!

thinks she's an RLS big shot.

Then it hit me!

(If this book were a comic strip, right now . . . at this exact moment . . . you'd see . . .)

BOING!

Cheesie Mack for Sixth-Grade President!

If I won the election, Goon would go bonkers! And that would probably generate a major victory for me in the Point Battle.

But could I win the election?

If I ran and lost, Goon would tease me forever (maybe longer!) about how she was really popular and I was a proven loser.

I was thinking hard about it when a door behind Mrs. Collins opened and a tall man with a buzz cut stepped out. The door had a nameplate on it that said MR. STEWART STOTTS, PRINCIPAL.

"Ed . . . ward Chap . . . ple," Mr. Stotts said as he took the wrinkled blue slip from the secretary. His tone wasn't stern, but the way he stretched out Eddie's name made it sound ominous. (Remember *ominous* from my first book? It means something bad is going to happen.)

"This has not been a good first day for you, Edward. Two blue slips in less than"—Mr. Stotts looked at the wall clock—"thirty minutes. Please take a seat in my office."

Eddie disappeared into the principal's office. Mr. Stotts looked at me. "Did you escort Edward?"

I nodded.

"Wait, please. He'll be with me for only one sentence." Mr. Stotts started toward his office, then looked at me again. "June Mack's your sister, right?"

I nodded again.

"She's quite an asset here at Stevenson," said Mr. Stotts. "Good student. Good citizen. Eighth-grade vice president."

Goon always seems to fool grown-ups. It's like she has some kind of magic power that makes her eviliciousness invisible to them.

Mr. Stotts patted me on the shoulder in a very uncle-ish way. "You must be very proud to be June Mack's little brother," he said, then walked back to his office.

That does it! I said to myself. *I am not going to be*

*known at RLS as June Mack's little brother! I'm going
to be Cheesie Mack, sixth-grade class president!*

I walked over to the bulletin board, took one of the
election registration forms, and stuck it in my pocket.
I wasn't trying to spy, but Mr. Stotts didn't bother to
close his office door, so I could see everything.

"I'll make it short, Eddie," Mr. Stotts said. He was
standing over Eddie, one hand running through his
buzz cut. "You've just bought yourself thirty days of
probation. One more blue slip during that time, and
you're suspended for a week. End of discussion. Back
to first period."

That was actually *five* sentences. But maybe Mr.
Stotts meant one sentence like the kind of sentence a
judge gives a convicted criminal.

*Edward Chapple, you are hereby sentenced to one
month in Probation Prison!*

"What'd you do this morning?" I asked Eddie as
we left the office. "The other blue slip, I mean."

"Skateboarding."

"In the school yard?" I was stunned. There were
NO SKATEBOARDING signs everywhere.

"Nope." He gave me an almost-smile. "In this hallway."

We passed by the recycling bin and turned into the corridor that led back to room 113. "It's none of my business," I said, "but you had to know that you'd get busted both times, right?"

Eddie stopped walking, so I did, too. "You're Ronald, right?" he asked.

"Everyone calls me Cheesie," I said.

"You're right, Cheesie. It's none of your business." Eddie stared at me just long enough to make me uncomfortable. Then he said, "But I'll tell you anyway. I went to Bass Rock Elementary. I don't know any of the kids from Goose Cove or Rocky Neck."

That made sense. Gloucester has three elementary schools, and they all send their kids to RLS. So most of us knew only about one-third of the kids.

"But now word'll get around," Eddie continued. "Everyone will know who Eddie Chapple is." He poked his thumbs into his chest for emphasis.

"In a bad way, maybe," I said.

"Nope." Eddie shook his head. "I didn't do anything bad. You tell me what's really bad about skateboarding and making a joke. It was funny, wasn't it?"

"Kinda."

"All I did was let everyone know that Eddie Chapple does things his own way."

"But what if you get another blue slip?" I asked. "You'll get suspended."

"I won't get another blue slip," Eddie said. "At least not before the election. You see, Cheesie, those two blue slips were all part of my plan. I'm going to run for class president."

He started walking again. I followed, my hand touching the election registration form in my pocket.

Me against Eddie Chapple?

I wasn't worried.

Yet.

Chapter 3

An Impossible Assignment

All the kids looked at us as we reentered room 113. Mrs. Wikowitz, on the other hand, was writing on the whiteboard and paid us no attention.

She turned to the class as Eddie and I took our seats. "When you submit a paper, or a report, or any homework at all, it must be in the proper format."

Everyone had a format sheet on three-hole paper. There was one on my desk.

Month Day, Year	**First Name Surname**
Mrs. Wikowitz	Core
	Assignment #_____
Title (if needed)	
Your work . . .	
	(if more than one page) Page #

"Please put this sample in your SuperBinders for reference," Mrs. Wikowitz said.

There was a lot of shuffling of paper and clicking of binder rings.

"If you do not follow the format exactly," she continued, "you will get an F on the assignment. And when I say 'exactly,' that is exactly what I mean. If you write the date without a comma, you will get an F. If you write your first name but omit your surname, you will get an F. If you forget page numbers on a multipage assignment, you will get an F."

She paused and looked around, but no one said anything.

"Good. Let's begin with assignment number one. Take out a sheet of lined paper and write one page describing as much as you can remember of what has occurred in this room, beginning with my entering and culminating now. We will do this silently and without asking any questions of me or other students. You may choose any writing style you feel is appropriate. You have fifteen minutes."

I frowned. There had been a whole chunk of time,

when Eddie and I had gone to the office, during which I hadn't been in the room. I raised my hand.

"No questions, Ronald."

I put my hand down, sat for a while trying to figure out how to do an impossible assignment, and then began writing.

What I Wrote

September 3   Ronald Mack

Mrs. Wikowitz   Core

                                        Assignment #1

Detective Armack's Report

I began my shift in room 113 at 8:12 a.m. I sat in the second row, surrounded by a small crowd, most of whom were strangers to me. On my right was a jagged young man identified by his name card as Edward Chapple. Since this was my first day on the job, I had no reason to suspect anything unusual was about to occur.

Into the room walked a tall woman dressed in dark

clothes. She began by introducing herself in writing, her silence creating tension.

Then, in a manner that showed control and authority, she directed the crowd, one by one, to read from a book of strange and unusual regulations. At first this proceeded without incident. My turn came. I handled it without difficulty. Then Mr. Chapple read . . . but not in English. It was no language I had ever heard.

The crowd reacted with amusement, but then everyone fell silent as the tall woman identified the young man as a criminal and asked me to take him into custody.

I left with the alleged perpetrator, and while we were gone, it is my conclusion, based upon biological principles previously known to me, that all the people in room 113 grew microscopically. I also conclude, due to my experience and subsequent observation, that all of them continued to breathe, probably normally, although I suspect, as the result of a previous investigation, that a young man with red-framed glasses held his breath once for thirty seconds for no obvious reason.

My understanding of the earth's rotation leads me to assume that daylight continued to come in through the windows, and my subsequent observation of the limited number of dust specks in the sun shafts suggests that the room had recently been vacuumed.

In the stomach of the young man with red-rimmed glasses, whom I had interrogated earlier that morning, a pancake breakfast was digesting and moving into his small intestines. Where it might go from there does not need further investigation.

When I returned with my prisoner, I was asked to file this report.

Signed: RLS Detective Armack

Since I had no idea what had actually happened in room 113 while I accompanied Eddie to the office, and Mrs. Wikowitz said we could choose any writing style, I decided to write assignment number one as a police detective. My dad, who reads police novels, has told me about *alleged perpetrator* and *interrogate,* which are police-talk for a) the person you suspect committed the crime and b) ask questions.

There's no place in Mrs. Wikowitz's report format for a chapter number. But the people who publish this book told me I had to call it something. So I used my homeroom and assignment numbers to make a police case number. You probably guessed how I came up with the name Armack.

Mrs. Wikowitz graded the papers while we read a short story.

I forgot to write the year in the upper left-hand corner.

I got an F.

Chapter 3½

(which is a continuation of Chapter 3)
Mulligans and Noogies

With only five minutes left in first period, Mrs. Wikowitz asked us to close our textbooks.

"The name of this school is . . ." She looked around the room. "George Sinkoff?"

"Robert Louis Stevenson Middle School," he replied quickly.

"And who was Robert Louis Stevenson?"

I knew he was a long-ago writer but didn't know what he wrote. I wasn't surprised when Georgie shrugged an I-don't-know.

"Anyone?" Mrs. Wikowitz asked.

Four hands went up, including Glenn's. I wasn't

surprised. I bet Glenn is the smartest sixth grader at RLS even though there are plenty of smart kids from the two other elementary schools.

The girl sitting next to me also had her hand up. Mrs. Wikowitz called on her. "Oddny Thorsdottir. Did I pronounce your name correctly?"

"Yes, ma'am," Oddny said. "Robert Louis Stevenson was a writer of fiction in the late nineteenth century. He is most famous for *Treasure Island* and *The Strange Case of Dr. Jekyll and Mr. Hyde*."

"Have you read either of those novels?"

"Yes, ma'am. Both."

"Good." The corner of Mrs. Wikowitz's mouth bent up. It might have been a tiny smile, but I wasn't sure. "You can help the rest of the class over the next few weeks as we read and discuss this one." She stood and passed out copies of *Treasure Island*. (When I showed it to Granpa that evening, he told me it was a "ripping good pirate yarn" with lots of "seafaring and treachery." *Treachery* is a really good word that means double-crossing.)

We read aloud from *Treasure Island* until the first

bell sounded. We could hear kids moving through the hall to their second-period classes, but since Core lasts for two periods, Mrs. Wikowitz paid no attention to the outside chatter.

She switched us from language arts to social studies and explained that our first topic would be ancient history, beginning with prehistoric humans. We spent the next chunk of time discussing how people lived back then. We talked about fire, tool making, hunting, and living in caves.

I was really enjoying Mrs. Wikowitz's class. Maybe you're wondering how I could enjoy getting an F on my first assignment. Well, I didn't enjoy that, and neither did most of my classmates. (Over half the class, including Georgie, got Fs for one reason or another.) But just before Core ended, Mrs. Wikowitz explained, "No matter how clear and direct I am about following the format exactly, every year, most students fail the first assignment." She picked up the stack of papers. "Who knows what a mulligan is?"

Georgie raised his hand. "It's the same thing as a

noogie except you clonk your knuckle on someone's forearm instead of their head."

Lots of the kids laughed. Mrs. Wikowitz didn't. She arched one eyebrow, then said, "Not so. It is an informal term from the game of golf for a do-over, a second chance. I am giving a mulligan to all those with Fs and will regrade their papers."

(If you have ever had a really excellent mulligan, go to my website and tell me about it.)

Then the bell rang, and everybody stood up to go to third-period class. As I gathered my stuff, I realized that even though I had known Mrs. Wikowitz for less than two hours, I needed to update my first

Not smiling (unfriendly)

Stands perfectly straight

Interesting

impressions. I still thought she was unfriendly, demanding, and no-nonsense, but now I had to add interesting. The double period had gone by really fast.

At the door of Mrs. Wikowitz's classroom I said goodbye to Georgie and watched him walk down the hall. Georgie and I had been in the same class every year since kindergarten. At RLS, however, Georgie and I only had Core and last-period physical education together. It was going to be weird being separated for most of the day! But our lunches were at the same time. And we would bike back and forth to school together.

Lana Shen and Glenn Philips were in *all* my classes (except Lana is in girls' PE). I was glad Glenn was in my classes. Lana . . . I'm not so sure.

I headed up the stairs for science. According to my class schedule (you saw it on page 16), my science class would be in room 220. A room in the 200s is on the second floor. Room 334 would be on the third floor, room 407 on the fourth floor, and room 8116 on the eighty-first floor . . . except RLS only has two floors!

When I got to room 220, Mr. Amato was waiting by the door, smiling at everyone who entered the science lab. Remember Mr. Amato? He was the very short, very round teacher who saw me digging through the recycling for Eddie's blue slip. Mr. Amato also has a shiny bald head.

"Please sit anywhere you wish," he said as we filed

into the classroom. When I passed by, he said, "Nice to see you again."

The first thing I noticed about the science lab was the posters covering the walls: a rocket ship blasting off, Saturn and its rings, a spider eating a moth (my favorite), an X-ray of a human head, and lots of famous scientists. Also, the desks were different from the ones in a normal classroom. The kids sat on tall chairs at long tables with black countertops and sinks. There was science equipment on the tables and all around the room: racks of test tubes, balance scales, glass beakers, rubber hoses hooked at one end to gas-supply knobs and to Bunsen burners at the other, and cabinets filled with bottles of chemicals.

I like experimenting. Sixth-grade science looked like it was going to be a fun class.

Mr. Amato closed the door and moved to the front of the room. "I do not use a seating chart," he said. Right away, I noticed that he is one of those people who talk with their hands. "One at a time (pointer finger in the air), please stand (both hands went up) and tell me your full name (arms went wide), and I shall memorize them (tapped his head)."

Mr. Amato pointed at Glenn, who was sitting in the front row on the end. "Let's start with you," he said.

Glenn stood. "Glenn Kareem Philips."

"Middle names are not necessary," Mr. Amato said, wagging a finger from side to side.

One by one, my classmates stood, said their names, and sat down. When the last kid sat down, Mr. Amato took a deep breath, put his forefinger to the side of his head like he was thinking really hard, looked at Glenn, and said, "Glenn Kareem Philips." He went down the rows, pointing at each student and saying that kid's name. When he got to Lana, he paused, started to call her Laura, then corrected himself and went on. Near the end he started going slower, but eventually he got every name correct, and the class cheered.

I just smiled because I knew he had tricked us. (How did I know? Just wait.)

Then Mr. Amato put on a long white lab coat and

did some really cool experiments—liquids changing color all by themselves, water disappearing as he poured it from one beaker to another, hammering a nail with a frozen banana, and blasting smoke rings out of a cardboard box all the way across the room! (Descriptions of these are on my website.)

Just before class ended, Mr. Amato hung up his lab coat and said, "In science one should never believe anything without proof." He laughed and waved both hands. "When class began, you witnessed me memorizing all your names. Right?"

Lots of kids nodded. I didn't.

"I have amazing mental powers, correct?" Mr. Amato tapped his shiny head with one forefinger, and then said, "Or do I? Is that what really happened?" He hunched up his shoulders and stuck both arms out wide.

I looked around. Everyone—even Glenn—seemed confused. Not me. Earlier that morning when I'd met him in the hall, he'd given himself away. I raised my hand.

"Aha!" he said with a grin. "Has Ronald Mack solved this mystery?"

I had.

I told him what I knew . . . and totally busted him! He laughed. Can you guess what I said? Turn to the next chapter for the answer.

Chapter 4

My Wet Butt

Did you notice the title of this chapter?

While I was writing the previous page, Georgie, who has been lying on my bed reading a science fiction novel, told me it's important for an author to grab the reader's attention when he starts a new chapter.

"How about calling the next part 'Attack of the Slime Monsters'?" Georgie suggested. "That would definitely get my attention."

He is right about chapter titles, but since I'm writing about what *actually* happened at the beginning of sixth grade—and there are no slime monsters at RLS (except maybe Goon!)—I will tell you instead about my drippy behind.

I hope you like it.

The chapter, I mean.

Not my drippy behind.

But first, here's the answer to Mr. Amato's trickery.

How did Mr. Amato memorize all the kids' names?

When I was in the hall digging through the recycling bin, it was the first time I had ever seen him and the first time he had ever seen me. But he said, "See you in third period," which means he recognized me and knew I was in his science class. Therefore he must have studied our photographs and memorized our names prior to the first day of school.

Fourth period was math. We reviewed fractions, percents, and areas of triangles. I was assigned to a group with Glenn, Lana, and a girl named Rita Pimental. Our teacher, Ms. Hammerbord, didn't say it, but if Glenn is in a group, it's the top group. Not bragging, but I'm good at math.

Lots happened at lunch.

Georgie and I met at the cafeteria door, just like we'd planned.

"Big news, Georgie," I told him confidentially. "I'm going to run for class president."

"Awesome," Georgie said. "I'm hungry."

Georgie is always hungry.

Both of us had brought lunch from home. Goon had been complaining for two years about how bad middle school food was, so we both decided we needed to check it out first. We passed by a table of girls from Rocky Neck. I ignored them (even though Lana was waving). Georgie and I sat on the far side of the room with Glenn Philips and two other boys from my math class. All three had purchased the school lunch—tacos, which looked delicious—and were already eating.

"How's the food?" I asked.

"Good," one kid mumbled, chomping big bites.

"Really good," the other boy said.

"Perfectly seasoned," Glenn offered. "I'm getting another." He stood up and got in line for seconds.

As usual, Goon had given me bad advice. Actually,

it's mostly my fault. She's a vegetarian, so I should've realized she wouldn't even have tasted most of the lunches.

When Glenn returned, he explained how different taste buds on your tongue sense different flavors: sweet is detected at the tip of the tongue, sour on the sides, etc. I had a pickle in my lunch, and Georgie had a hunk of fudge, so I tested my taste buds by touching pieces of them to various parts of my tongue. As usual, Glenn was right. If you want to try this yourself, I put a taste bud diagram on my website.

Georgie and I finished eating quickly and decided to explore the school for the remainder of the lunch period. As we stood up, Goon motioned to me from a table on the other side of the cafeteria. Instead of ignoring her as I should have done, I walked over. Georgie followed. When I got close, my Goon-Alarm began clanging loudly inside my head because both she and her boyfriend, Drew, were grinning big-time.

"Sit down. I have something important to tell you," Goon said, pointing to the empty chair next to her.

I plopped down, and wet my pants.

NOT!

I (Cheesie) did not wet my pants. Goon wet my pants. She had poured water into the hollowed-out part of the chair, and I sat in it.

Most kids would've yelped or made a face or jumped up or something. I didn't. Even though she had tricked me, I was instantly and completely aware of the Point Battle. If I got embarrassed and she saw that, she'd win points, doubled because other kids in the cafeteria would laugh. So I sat absolutely still (even though cold water was soaking through to my underwear) and said, "What's up?"

She stared at me. Her nose got all wrinkly and her eyebrows got all bunchy. If I had a brain-wave translator, I bet I would've heard her thinking, *Huh? Why isn't he screaming? I know I put water there.*

"What'd you want to tell me?" I continued.

"Stand up," Goon said.

"Stand up," Drew repeated. Goon's boyfriends always seem to do whatever she says.

I didn't move. "You just told me to sit down. C'mon, what'd you want?"

"Stand up," she insisted.

"Do what she says," Drew said.

"You guys are just messing with me," I replied, turning away. "Georgie, grab a chair. Let's work on the vocabulary for Mrs. Wikowitz."

"Do we have an assignment?" Georgie asked.

"We have to come up with some new words." I slid a napkin to him and winked so that Goon couldn't see. "Remember?"

"Oh, yeah. Vocab. Thanks for reminding me." Georgie pulled over a chair from the next table and sat down next to me. He pulled a pen out of his pocket.

Of course we didn't have any such assignment. But Georgie knew I was up to something and played along. That's what is great about having a best friend.

"Stand up!" Goon yelled in my ear. She screeched so loudly, a teacher standing two tables away looked over.

I ignored Goon. "I just thought of a good word. How about *obtuse*?" I said to Georgie. "It's a math word, but you can use it in other ways."

Georgie nodded, wrote the word on the napkin, and showed it to me. "Is this how you spell it?"

"Uh-huh." I glanced at my sister. She was puffing and huffing, which meant she was getting flustered and agitated.

"What's the definition?" Georgie asked.

"It's a perfect description of the people around us," I said, not looking at my sister on purpose. "Just write *simpleminded* and *thickheaded,* with a semicolon in between."

That pushed Goon over the edge. She jumped up, shouted, "You're an idiot!" and tried to tip me out of my seat. Drew jumped up, too.

"Stop it!" I yelled, knocking her hand off the back

of my chair. Almost immediately the teacher who'd noticed us before came over to our table.

"What's going on here?" he asked. I didn't know it then, but it was Coach T, my PE teacher.

Goon immediately backed away and mumbled, "Nothing. He's my stupid brother, and he's a stupid jerk."

"I'm just trying to do my homework," I said innocently.

"This family argument is now over," Coach T said. "Time to make nice."

Goon blushed. Not a lot, but I saw it.

Point Battle victory!

"Why don't you move along and leave your brother alone?" the coach continued.

Goon gave me a super-mean look, spun around, and stormed out of the cafeteria. Drew followed at her heels just the way my dog, Deeb, follows me.

Coach T gave me a look like he was waiting for me to say something.

"It's vocabulary stuff," Georgie explained, pointing at the napkin with his pen.

Coach T nodded and went back to his post.

"Wow! What flew up your sister's nose?" Georgie asked.

"I'll show you in a minute," I said. Without getting out of my chair, I took off my sweatshirt and tied it around my waist. Then I stood up. "Follow me."

I walked quickly to the boys' bathroom, lifted my sweatshirt, and turned my butt toward Georgie.

His eyebrows shot upward. "Holy moly! What'd you do? No, don't tell me!"

"It's not what you think," I said. Then I told him the whole story. What I didn't tell him, because not even Georgie knows about the Point Battle, was that I had turned an eight-point wet-butt loss into a four-point victory. The Point Battle score was now 694–677.

Chapter 5

Running for President

I sat on my sweatshirt all through fifth-period Spanish. *Al momento que la clase terminó* (by the time the class was over), my pants had gone from drippy to barely damp. In a way, it was a science experiment. I had proven that body heat can help dry out clothes.

When I got to the PE locker room for my final class of the day, I changed into shorts and an RLS T-shirt. Then I joined the rest of the boys in the gym, where we sat in the stands. Coach T had switched from his teacher clothes to sweatpants and a T-shirt with GEORGETOWN written on it. (That's a university in Washington, DC. They usually have a good basketball team. I looked it up.)

"My name is Coach Tunavelov," the coach said. If you want to know what Coach T looked like, imagine what a PE coach would look like if you were watching a movie about a PE coach. Big, strong, square-jawed—that's Coach T.

He turned sideways like he was talking to an imaginary guy next to him and said, "Why is there a fish on the floor?"

Then he faced the other way. "Because the 'tuna fell off' the table."

It took us a minute, but then everyone laughed—the coach was making a joke about his name. He smiled.

"Look, Tunavelov is a fine Slavic name," he said. "But it's a mouthful, so you're going to call me Coach T. And by the way, I've heard every fish joke in the world, so don't even try."

Everybody nodded.

(I have not heard every fish joke in the world, so if you know any good ones, please go to my website and tell me. I'm building a collection.)

"If you call me teacher or teach or mister—or if I hear a fish joke—you'll be doing push-ups. It's Coach T. Got it?"

Alex Welch raised his hand. "I have two questions. Can we call you Mister Coach? And what does the T stand for?"

Alex was not trying to be funny. He just sounds like a dope sometimes.

Coach T gave him a long, hard look.

Uh-oh, I thought, *here come a thousand push-ups.* But Coach T just sighed and turned back to the rest of us. Maybe, like Mrs. Wikowitz, he was giving Alex a first-day mulligan.

"All right, listen up. The elementary school phys ed you boys did last year was just a bunch of horsing around. Now you're sixth graders, and you're going to do things the right way. The Coach T way." He lifted both arms and flexed his muscles. "Let's get started on your baseline physical fitness test."

For the rest of the period we did chin-ups, sit-ups, and push-ups, and climbed a rope. He and another PE teacher wrote down what everybody did.

I had never done the rope climb before. And maybe you haven't either. Here's how it works. A rope hangs from the ceiling. You have to climb the rope using your hands and feet, touch a small plastic ball twelve feet up, and then come back down.

I did great because I'm strong and light. It's harder for big guys. They weigh too much.

"Go, Georgie!" I shouted when it was his turn. Georgie is really big, but he's also really strong. It took him a while, but he made it to the top.

"Good job, Sinkoff!" Coach T said. I saw him put a big check mark next to Georgie's name.

Then it was Glenn Philips's turn. He's never been very interested in sports, but he scampered up the rope like a monkey. Afterward he told me, "I intend to increase my physical prowess this year." (*Prowess* means skill or expertise. Glenn has an excellent vocabulary.)

The last thing we did was shoot free throws.

"Basketball is not part of the baseline physical fitness test," Coach T announced, "but I intend to have a winning season. Let's see how you guys do."

Eddie Chapple made four out of five. (I was not surprised. Remember his wadded blue-slip toss?) Georgie made three. I made none. Neither did Glenn.

Since one of our math homework problems was to do a survey of something and put the results into a bar chart, I asked Coach T for the free throw data. Here's what I turned in to Ms. Hammerbord the next day.

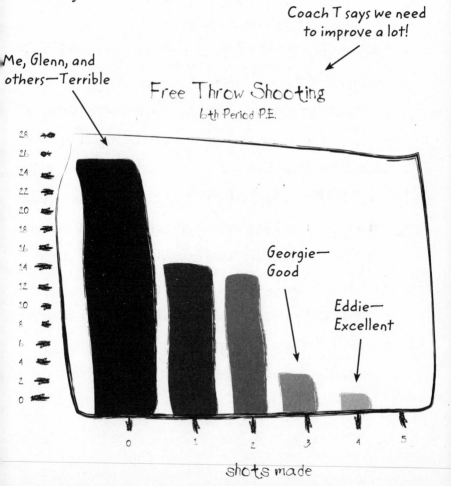

Coach T says we need to improve a lot!

Me, Glenn, and others—Terrible

Free Throw Shooting
6th Period P.E.

Georgie— Good

Eddie— Excellent

shots made

After class was over and we were back in the locker room changing into our regular clothes, Georgie said, "I'd like to have a basketball hoop in my driveway, but my dad thinks I'd break windows."

"You broke two already," I said. I wasn't being mean. It was a fact. Georgie can really peg a baseball.

"Your fault. You could've caught both of them."

"Yeah, if I had an extendo-arm."

Georgie ignored me. "If I could practice free throws at home, I bet I could make five out of five."

"Yeah, probably," I replied. Maybe you think he was bragging, but Georgie was just telling the truth. He's a terrific athlete.

"We have a basketball hoop at our house," Alex Welch said, jumping out from behind a row of lockers where he'd obviously been eavesdropping. "I'm going to practice until I can do six out of five."

"I'll buy you a gold-plated, diamond-studded basketball if you do that," Georgie said.

"Really?" Alex replied.

Georgie just grinned.

On our bike ride home from school we talked about our classes.

"That new girl Oddny sits next to me in science," Georgie said.

"What does that have to do with anything?" I asked.

"Race you home!" he replied, and pumped hard.

I won.

At dinner that evening I was ready to make the big announcement that I was running for class president, so I picked up my fork, waved it dramatically in the air, and began. "I have something big to—"

But suddenly Goon zipped in from washing her hands, slid into her seat, and interrupted. "Hold it! You guys have to hear this first!" She gave me an I-just-cut-in-front-of-you-ha-ha look.

I kept my mouth shut and dug a trench in my mashed potatoes.

"In my ballet class, I'm trying out for a show in Boston. It takes place over Christmas vacation."

She began bouncing up and down in her chair.

"They're only picking one girl. If I win, I get to

stay in a college dorm for a week. And I get to dance in *The Nutcracker*! Onstage! In Boston!"

"That's terrific, sweetheart," Mom said.

Goon rocked her head back and forth happily. "All I have to do now is write an essay. It's due in a few days."

I scooped a huge glob of mashed potatoes into my mouth and sat there with my cheeks puffed out like a chipmunk's.

"You're a shoo-in," Granpa stated. "Dancing talent is thick in this family. My sister danced her way across Europe after the war."

My dad chimed in. "Her feet must've been plenty tired by the time she got to Czechoslovakia, Pop." Then Dad gave me a squinty-evil-eye.

I tried to swallow. "I hope you win," I said potato-fully to Goon.

"Shut up," Goon said.

I'm willing to bet "shut up" is the phrase Goon says to me most.

I swallowed. "No, really. I really hope you win."

Everyone was staring at me, trying to figure out

what I was up to. But I wasn't up to anything. If there was a chance for Goon to be absent for a whole week during winter break, I was all for it!

Finally Mom turned back to Goon and smiled. "It would be a perfect reward for all the hard work you've put in."

Goon does practice ballet a lot.

At last it was my turn. "I have an announcement, too. I have decided to run for sixth-grade class president."

Mom looked surprised. Dad looked surprised. Granpa grinned. Goon choked on a bite of carrot. Dad had to slap her on the back to dislodge it. When she finally stopped coughing, she was so upset she could barely speak.

"Mom, no! Dad! You have to . . . I mean . . . make him not do it. You cannot imagine . . . it's so embarrassing . . . having him in my school. No. Please!"

Mom gave Goon a stern look. "First, it's not *your* school. Ronald is a student there, too. Second, you should be proud that your brother is ambitious. And third, if he wins—"

"*When* he wins!" Granpa interrupted. "My grandson is a born leader. It comes with being a Mack."

Mom continued, "When he wins, you'll both be in the student government meetings, and perhaps you can take advantage of those occasions to learn to work together harmoniously."

I hadn't thought of that. I would have to be in the same room as Goon.

Bad news.

From the look on Goon's face, I could tell she felt exactly, precisely, definitely, completely, and utterly the same way about that as I did. She once told me she didn't like breathing the same air as me.

I ate the rest of my dinner in silence. Later that evening I was in my room doing homework when Goon came to my door.

"Hey," she said.

"What?"

"I'm sorry I was so negative about your running for class president."

Huh? I was instantly on my guard. Goon almost

never apologizes to me. And she was carrying a big, rolled-up sheet of paper.

"I made this poster for you," she said, taping it on the inside of my door. "Good luck."

She was up to something.

I went to bed mulling (a good school word; it means thinking about something deeply and at length) the pros and cons of running. Here's what I came up with:

1. In order to win I'd have to get to know lots more sixth graders. I'd probably end up with a bunch of new friends. PRO.

2. Goon would do things to try to make me look stoopid. (That's my made-up word that means "really stupid," because it's a really stupid way of spelling *stupid*.) CON.

3. It would be fun to be class president. PRO.

4. Goon is a very tricky girl. She knows the ins and outs of RLS and student government way better than I do. She would succeed (I know she would, she's super devious) in making me look stoooopid (an even stupider word for *stupid*). CON.

My list came out even, so I pulled my pillow over my head. Maybe I wouldn't run for president.

Chapter 6

Cheesie Gets Socked

The next two days were super busy. I had to:

1. Get used to my new teachers. (Señora Lunares speaks *only* Spanish in class!)

2. Start a drawing project in art. (I'm terrible.)

3. Help Mr. Amato organize his science supplies and put them into the drawers and cabinets in the science lab. (He picked me for the extra credit because I was the only kid to figure out his memory trick.)

4. Do more homework than I ever had in elementary school. (At least the math isn't hard.)

There was so much stuff going on, I completely forgot about the decision I had to make.

Then Goon made up my mind by sabotaging me.

I had just come out of the bathroom after my morning shower and there she was, trespassing in my bedroom.

"Get out!" I yelled.

As she ran past me back out into the hall, I could see she was carrying an armload of my socks. I chased her but gave up halfway down the stairs. I am much faster than Goon, but think about it . . . how fast and

how far can you run when all you've got on is a towel?

Once back in my room, I discovered she had:

1. Torn up the election registration form I'd gotten in the school office.
2. Used her markers to color my SuperBinder pink and purple.
3. Taken exactly half the socks out of my dresser.

I threw on some pants and stomped downstairs. As soon as Goon heard me coming, she dashed out the door for school. Mom——she's an air-traffic controller at the airport——was already gone, and Dad was just pulling out of the driveway on one of his limousine jobs.

Granpa was reading the newspaper. "Don't look at me, kiddo," he said. "A stinking pile of squabble is the last thing I'm interested in first thing in the morning." He stared at me, no squinty-evil-eye. "You're a big boy, Cheesie. Handle it."

I looked down at my bare feet and thought, *Good advice, Granpa. I know exactly what I'll do. Goon will not get points for this.*

Ten minutes later Georgie and I were riding our bikes to school.

"I was thinking about your class president campaign," Georgie shouted to me over the noise of passing traffic. "You could totally win. Especially if I'm your campaign manager. We'll put up posters. We'll use your grandfather's camera to make a video just like real politicians do. And we'll get the video on the school's TV station."

I didn't respond. I was thinking about how upset Goon would be the next time she saw me.

Georgie didn't notice. "I wonder how much it would cost to buy 'Cheesie for President' buttons," he continued. "We could hand them out all over school."

When we stopped at a red light, Georgie looked down at my feet. "Why are you wearing different-colored socks?"

"Goon," I said, pulling up my pant legs to show one red and one blue sock. "She stole every sock that matched."

Georgie made a what-are-you-gonna-do face.

"But," I said with a grin, "when she tries to

tease me, I'll just say 'You lose! These are RLS school colors.' "

The light turned green.

"That's perfect for your campaign!" Georgie shouted as he pedaled across Main Street.

Huh? I thought as I zoomed after him.

Georgie smiled at me and didn't say anything for one long block. I could tell he was thinking up another of his Great Ideas.

"You are so lucky to have me as your campaign manager," he said as we pedaled past bunches of kids walking to school, "because you know what wins school elections?" He was so excited he began twisting his handlebars back and forth and zigzagging down the street. "School spirit, that's what. Starting today, you're going to be *Mr. Cheesie RLS School Spirit*. You're going to wear something red and something blue every day until the election!"

Sometimes Georgie's Great Ideas are Great. Sometimes they are Not So Great. This one was, IMO, Really Really Great. It would turn Goon's trickery, and my school colors idea, into something even better for me. When we coasted into the school's bicycle parking area, I was grinning big-time.

"Campaigns need slogans," I said as we locked our bikes and entered the building. We began fast-walking to class. The halls were full of kids, so we weren't even close to being tardy. We just felt like speed-walking.

Georgie thought for a moment, then said, "How about 'Cheesie Will Stand Up for RLS. He Won't Melt'? You know, like melted cheese?"

Georgie made a big fake-smile.

I gave him an ugh-face as we sped toward our homeroom. Mrs. Wikowitz was standing just inside the door. When Georgie stepped around her, his backpack crashed into me. For someone who is a terrific athlete, he can be such a klutz!

"All right. Here's a better one," he said as we approached Lana's front-row desk. She waved to me. She always does that.

Just to be polite, I gave her the littlest wave back, but I was listening to Georgie.

"How about 'Cheesie Doesn't Stink'?" Georgie

continued. "You know, like stinky cheese."

"That stinks," I said.

"Okay . . . how about—"

"What're you guys talking about?" Lana asked.

Before I could *not* answer (I wasn't going to tell her that I was running for president yet), she interrupted herself.

"Omigosh, Cheesie. What happened to your SuperBinder?"

I said one word: "Goon."

"I can fix it for you, if you want," she said.

I shrugged, looked at Georgie, and shrugged again. Lana dug into her backpack and took out tape, colored paper, and scissors. Cut . . . tape . . . cut . . . tape . . . cut . . . tape, and the pink-and-purple DOOFUS, DWEEB, and DORK-BOY SuperBinder was completely covered with orange construction paper.

"That's your favorite color," Lana said as she handed back my binder.

I'd never told her that. How did she know?

(I'm doing a favorite-color survey on my website. What's yours?)

"Um, thanks," I said.

Lana smiled and sat back down.

The bell rang, and Mrs. Wikowitz began the class by collecting permission forms for a field trip we were taking the next day to Minute Man National Historical Park. Then she handed back the assignments she'd regraded from the first day. In red ink at the bottom of mine, she'd written: *Det. Armack is an intriguing and observant character. Good work!* A.

Hooray for mulligans!

Several hours later I was standing behind Georgie in the lunch line. "After we eat I'm going to the office to get another election registration form," I said to the back of his head.

But Georgie wasn't listening. He was totally focused on convincing the lunch lady to give him a double helping of fish nuggets. (We often have them in our schools because fish nuggets were supposedly invented in Gloucester.)

I like fish nuggets, but I was in the mood for mac 'n' cheese. When I walked past Goon's table with my tray, she snarked, "Nice socks, Runtboy."

Maybe she thought I'd be embarrassed, but no way! I just smiled and replied, "School colors, loser."

As I walked away, I heard Drew mumble, "Cool idea."

"It's stupid!" Goon said loudly.

I glanced back. She might have sounded tough, but her embarrassed expression told me she knew her sock-stealing plan had backfired. I awarded myself four Point Battle points. The score was 694–681!

I ate lunch with a big grin on my face, sort of sticking my feet out to show off my school-color ankles. At first no one noticed. Then some girls walked by, and one of them, Kandy DeLeon (I have never mentioned Kandy before, but she was in my fifth-grade class), made a big deal about my socks. I explained about the school-color thing, and pretty soon a whole group of girls was hanging around and chattering.

Kandy was sort of jumping from foot to foot. "That's so cool! Hey, everyone, look at Cheesie's socks! We should definitely have a sixth-grade school-colors day." Kandy has excellent school spirit and also a loud voice.

I looked over at Goon. She was steaming. Ha!

I didn't award myself more Point Battle points, though. An embarrassment only counts once.

"We could do it every week," said a girl voice behind me.

I knew instantly who it was. I turned around. It was Lana, standing there with Oddny. I had a glop of mac 'n' cheese on my spork, so I shoved it into my mouth. (I think the spork is a great invention, and a cool word. A foon is the same thing, but who wants to eat with a foon?)

Another girl from my fifth-grade class, Livia Grant, singsonged, "Cheesie Mack eats mac 'n' cheese."

Very original.

Oddny sat down beside Georgie. "Hello, Georgie.

You wanted to ask me something about our science homework?"

Georgie gave me an I-have-to-do-this look and struggled to pull a wad of paper from his pocket. He flattened it on the table, slid it in front of Oddny, and read his terrible handwriting aloud: "*Algae, fungi, microorganism, bacteria, protozoa.* What're we supposed to do with these words?"

Georgie and I have science during different periods, but we both have Mr. Amato. I had done that assignment last night.

Why did he ask Oddny instead of me? I wondered. *Weird.*

Lana slid in next to me. I slid a little bit away from her—I don't like people sitting too close to me while I'm eating. When Oddny finished explaining the microbiology terms to Georgie, I pointed to my food. "Mr. Amato said microorganisms are everywhere," I said.

"I bet there's algae, fungi, bacteria, and proto-zo-zos in this."

I sporked up the last macaroni on my plate. "Proto-zo-zos," I repeated. (Some words, especially made-up ones, are fun to say out loud.)

"Gross," Lana said, but she was smiling like she thought I was funny.

I stood. "See you last period, Georgie. I gotta go to the office."

"Why?" Lana asked.

"None of your beeswax," I said. (Granpa taught me that phrase. I think kids used to say it when he was little.)

Georgie and I had decided not to talk about my campaign until it was official. But then I noticed that Lana looked like I'd hurt her feelings, so I changed to a very sneaky, spy-guy voice. "Top-secret stuff. I'll tell you soon."

Lana grinned. Then Oddny started explaining about microorganisms to Georgie, and I remembered something I'd read about certain kinds of mites. Mites are related to ticks and are in the same animal class as spiders. They're bigger than microorganisms, but most are too small to see without a microscope.

"Hey, Georgie," I said as I picked up my tray. "Why don't you show Oddny your demodex mites?"

Georgie knew what I was talking about, so he laughed. Oddny and Lana looked confused. I walked away grinning.

Get ready to be grossed out!

Most people—maybe even you!—have lots of tiny mites on their faces. These creatures live in the pores at the bottom of your eyelashes and eat dead skin and oil.

(I bet some of you are going "Eeeeew!")

And even if you wash really hard, you can't get rid of them. They're crawling around your eyelids right now!

Eeeeew!

I wrote a demodex report for Mr. Amato's science class. It's on my website. But I warn you, I yanked out one of Georgie's eyelashes and looked at it through his microscope. GROSS!

When I got to the office, I filled out the election

registration form and handed it to the school secretary. I was starting to leave when a thought hit me.

"Um, can you tell me who else is running?" I asked her. "You know . . . my opponents?"

Mrs. Collins peered at me through her thick glasses, smiled, and began shuffling through a small stack of registration forms. As she sorted them into piles, she said, "Vice president . . . secretary . . . vice president . . . president . . . treasurer . . ."

When she finished, my registration form and three others were in the president pile. I am very good at reading upside down. I already knew who my opponents were before she picked up the papers and read the names to me.

Eddie Chapple. No surprise. He'd already told me he was running.

Diana Mooney. I'd never heard of her.

The last name was a big surprise, and one that would make things difficult for me.

Lana Shen.

Chapter 7

Running in the Zone

I was sitting next to Glenn Philips, putting on my PE clothes and thinking hard about my Lana Shen problem when Georgie bounced into the locker room.

"Cheesie, old friend, old pal, I am definitely going to get an A in science this year!" he said.

This was a surprising comment. Georgie is not usually an A student. He is plenty smart enough to get As, but he is lots of times lazy and sloppy about homework, and he gets way too nervous during tests.

Georgie opened his locker and began to change clothes. "That new girl, Oddny. I sit next to her in Mr. Amato's class. She is really smart." He looked over at Glenn. "Maybe as smart as you, Glenn, when it comes to science. Really smart."

Glenn shrugged. Georgie put his right foot into his left sneaker, realized his mistake, kicked the sneaker straight into the air, and caught it with his left foot. He is super good at things like that.

"She will definitely get an A in science," Georgie continued, pulling his RLS T-shirt over his head. "And she told me last period she's going to make sure I get an A, too!"

"Uh-oh," I said softly.

He paused, his head half through the T-shirt neck hole. "What?"

"Nothing."

One second later he had me in a headlock. "What?!"

I squirmed free, jumped away, and scooted toward the locker room door. "I think Oddny likes you!"

Georgie ran after me. "Of course she does. I know that. I can't help it if I'm way too handsome."

Outside, Coach T assembled our class at the running track that circles the combination football and soccer field. He waved an arm at the cloudless

September sky. "Another benchmark test on this beautiful day, boys. We're going to run a mile. That's four times around the track."

Lots of guys groaned or moaned.

"Mellow out, boys," Coach T said. "I don't care how fast you do it. What I'm looking for is heart, guts, and stamina. Can you do a mile without walking, stopping, or throwing up?"

As he lined us up, I wondered how I'd do. I'm a good runner—I knew that—but I had never run a mile before. I looked over at Georgie. I wondered if he could do a mile without stopping. He had a smile on his face. It was as if he knew what I was thinking.

"Don't worry about me, Cheesie," he said. "I'll do the whole mile. No problem. But you're going to be lots faster than me—"

Just then Coach T yelled, "GO!"

Fifty-six boys took off running. By the time I reached the first turn, the group was spread way out. Eddie Chapple was leading everyone by about ten yards. I was near the front with about a dozen guys, most of whom had come from the other elementary schools. Only Glenn Philips and I had gone to Rocky Neck. Georgie was somewhere in the middle, clumped up in a big pack.

When my near-the-front group passed Coach T the first time (lap #1), Glenn was still hanging with me. I was impressed. All through elementary school he'd been the littlest kid in class and always nonathletic, but over the summer he'd begun getting some kind of hormone shots that helped him grow a couple of inches and made him way stronger. (Remember his being like a monkey on the rope climb?)

By the time I passed Coach T again (lap #2 . . . we'd done a half mile), Eddie's lead had shrunk to ten feet, and only five kids were in the front pack. Glenn had dropped back into the middle group. I was breathing hard, but I was okay.

A few seconds later the front group caught up with the slowest guys in our class. They were now walking, which Coach T had said you weren't supposed to do, but I guess they were either too tired or, as Granpa would say, "dead-flat lazy." I, on the other hand, was really into the run. I began focusing on changing my breathing from hard panting to breathing long and slowly. I passed about a dozen guys.

Halfway through the third lap, Eddie and the rest of us in the lead had settled into a regular pace. My breathing was now strong and steady, but I had never run a mile before. Could I run that far without stopping?

By the time we passed Coach T a third time, all my outside thoughts had disappeared. It was kind of like I had gotten into a groove. I wasn't tired or out of breath or hurting. I was unaware of anything other than blue sky and cool air and the feel of my shoes on the track. My running seemed effortless. I felt like I could go forever. (My dad later told me it's called "being in the zone.")

Eddie was still a couple of strides ahead of me. It was just us two. The rest of the PE class was now spread out around the oval track. Eddie and I were passing lots of other boys.

With about a half lap to go, Eddie began to speed up. Until then, I hadn't been thinking about beating him. I had just been running. Nothing more than that.

And then I lapped Georgie. He shouted, "Go, Cheesie! Punch it!"

I punched it!

I came out of the zone and was suddenly aware. Up until then my ears had been mostly closed to outside sounds. Now I heard everything. Each breath was an explosion. Each footstep was a thud. And the voices of the other boys were a cacophony (ka-KAW-phony . . . my mom gave me that word . . . it means crazy, mixed-up noise) of cheers and shouts.

Step by step I gained on Eddie until only a few feet separated us. He looked over his shoulder. About fifty yards ahead I could see Coach T at the finish line. He had his hand raised, a stopwatch poised.

"Come on, boys!" he shouted.

I have a perfect memory of the last twenty yards of the run. There are no photos to prove this, but I know during those last few moments my face was scrunched into a grimace of determination. I caught up to Eddie, and for the next several strides we matched leg to leg,

our arms pumping up and down in unison. As we crossed the finish line, Coach T brought his hand down and clicked the stopwatch off.

Eddie and I staggered a little ways down the track, then sort of stumbled onto the infield and collapsed on the grass, trying to catch our breath.

"Good race," I panted in Eddie's general direction.

"Yeah," he panted back. "Who won?"

I opened my eyes. Coach T was standing over us, shaking his stopwatch in our faces. "I'd need a photo-finish camera to figure that out. Six minutes and nine seconds. Darn good time, boys. Really darn good time for this early in the year. Both of you are going to be on the cross-country team. I won't take no for an answer." He walked back toward the track, muttering, "Wow! Six minutes and nine seconds. Wow."

I rolled closer to Eddie. "I didn't know I could run that far or that fast."

"Me neither," he replied, his breathing still rasping out.

I lay there, feeling my heart pounding hard. I felt

terrific. "Hey, Eddie, I got some news. I'm running against you for class president."

"Oh, yeah?" he said, turning on his side to face me. "Don't get your hopes up. That won't be like this race. You don't stand a chance."

Chapter 8

Sinkoff for President!

That afternoon Georgie and I had some yard work to do at Ms. Prott's house (remember her and the Haunted Toad from my first book?), so we rode our bikes there. We raked up piles of leaves, had some juice and cookies at a table in her backyard, and listened to her tell a really terrific story about being an Army nurse in India during World War II. (It's on my website.)

As we rode our bikes home, I told Georgie who else was running for president.

"I know Diana Mooney," he said. "She's in my math class. She went to Goose Cove last year."

I looked over at him. He already knew what I was going to ask.

"She's really popular," Georgie said.

We pulled up at the Main Street stoplight.

"And a huge chatterbox," he continued, making a talking-mouth hand motion. "She'll get lots of votes, especially from kids who went to Goose Cove."

I shook my head. "This is bad, Georgie. Most kids are going to vote for the candidate who went to their school. Eddie went to Bass Rock. That leaves me and Lana with Rocky Neck. We're going to hurt each other's chances by splitting those votes."

The light changed. We rode across the street in silence. On the opposite side, Georgie stopped short and grabbed my arm.

"There's only one way you can win this election. You have to convince Lana *not* to run."

"How am I going to do that?"

"I'll show you. Follow me!"

He took off, but in the wrong direction. "Where're you going?" I yelled, pedaling after him. "Georgie?"

Then it hit me!

"GEORGIE!" I screamed.

He stopped and looked back at me.

"Come on!" Georgie shouted.

"No way! I am *not* going to Lana's house."

He stood astride his bike for a few moments, then rode slowly back to me.

"Do you want to be president or not?" he asked.

"I'll talk to her tomorrow. At school."

"Yeah?" Georgie said. "With all her friends around? 'Oh, look, everybody. Cheesie's talking to Lana. He likes Lana!' That's what they'll say. This way's private. We drop in and ask her to quit. Simple. Clean. In and out."

I stared at him for a moment and made a face. "I don't even know where she lives. How do you know?"

"Duh. Birthday party last year?" He began pedaling again. Reluctantly, I followed.

I recognized Lana's house when we turned onto her block. Mrs. Shen was in the driveway, lifting bags of groceries out of her car.

"Is Lana home?" Georgie asked as we laid our bikes down on the lawn.

"She's inside," Mrs. Shen replied, smiling broadly.

Now I remembered Lana's party. It was all about

hats. Sounds weird and maybe boring, huh? But no. It was really fun. Lana and her mom had bought a whole bunch of hats at Goodwill and Salvation Army, and everyone got to choose one (there were lots of different styles, way more than just baseball caps). Then we decorated them with tons of arts and crafts stuff. When we were done, we named our creations, put them on, and Mr. Shen judged them and gave out awards.

Mine was a white sailor's hat with globs of different-colored slime and goo hanging off it. I called it Sea Sickness. Mr. Shen had just come home from his job at the post office and looked like a very official

judge because he was still wearing his uniform. He awarded me a blue ribbon for Most Disgusting.

We helped Mrs. Shen carry her groceries.

"Lana," she called out as we entered the house. "You have company."

Lana was in the kitchen with Oddny. *Oh, darn,* I thought. I didn't want witnesses.

"We're baking muffins. Want some?" Lana said brightly, sliding a pan into the oven.

"Sure/no," Georgie and I said simultaneously.

For the next fifteen minutes we sat in the kitchen. Lana and Oddny chattered about school and friends and everything else. Georgie kind of participated. I kept quiet. It was weird. Lana never once asked why we were there. It was as if we always dropped by unannounced.

Finally the delicious baking smell told us the muffins were ready. There were twelve. We ate them piping hot with cold milk. Georgie was picking up his fourth when I spoke.

"Lana, remember when I went to the office today?"

She nodded.

"It was because, just like you, I'm running for class president."

"Oh," she said softly.

"I'm his campaign manager," Georgie said between muffin bites.

Then I told Lana how Diana Mooney and Eddie Chapple would probably grab most of the Goose Cove and Bass Rock ballots.

"And that's the problem. Both of us can't run. We'll just split the Rocky Neck votes and lose. So . . ."

I paused to take a gulp of milk. I knew what I was planning to say next, but while I was talking, I was looking at her . . . and she seemed sort of sad . . . and something happened as my words came out.

"I'm not going to run for class president."

A piece of muffin dropped from Georgie's mouth.

"If only one of us is going to run, you should do it," I continued.

For the next few moments each of us kind of just looked at the others. Lana and Oddny didn't know what to say. Georgie was completely confused. And I had no idea why I had done that.

It was really awkward.

(*Awkward* is a really awkward word. Look at the letters. Two *w*'s with a *k* in the middle. Weird. Plus an auk is a seabird. If you could teach it to speak, I bet its speech would be awkward. It's a joke, get it? *Auk word*.)

Finally Lana broke the awkward silence. "No, Cheesie. You'd have a much better chance to win. I won't run."

"That's crazy," I blurted, sitting up straight. "You've got a great personality. Kids will vote for you. And you'd make a way better president than me. You know how to do things."

"That's not true," she countered. "And everyone at Rocky Neck liked you. More than me, I think. You should run."

"No, you should run."

"You should," she said, pointing a finger at me.

"No, you!" I replied louder.

"No, you!" Lana yelled.

And then all four of us laughed. Muffin crumbs fell out of Georgie's mouth.

"I've got the answer," Oddny said suddenly, jumping up and waving her arms. "Neither one of you will run for class president. How about we all work together and elect Georgie?"

Georgie's muffin-mouth fell open. I looked at Lana. She stared at me. Then we both grinned.

"Sinkoff for president!" I yelled.

Chapter 9

The Bus Ride of Paul Revere

My decision not to run for class president was huge news in my house at dinner. I switched around what Mom, Dad, Granpa, Goon, and Deeb said. Can you guess who said what? Turn the page to see the answers.*

1. "OMG! That's the absolute best news I've ever heard."

2. "It would've been a good experience for you, but if you're sure you've thought this through . . ."

3. Gave me a squinty-evil-eye, but when I didn't smile, whispered, "Georgie's lucky to have you as a friend."

4. "Throw me a tennis ball." *(translated)*
5. "Big mistake! I know how these things work. You were a shoo-in."

The next morning, as we had planned the night before, Lana and Oddny were waiting at the RLS bike rack when Georgie and I pedaled in. The entire sixth grade was in the parking lot, boarding buses for our field trip.

"You guys run to the office and get Georgie's registration form!" Oddny shouted, dashing for the bus our homeroom was boarding. "I'll save us seats!"

Lana, Georgie, and I sprinted past teachers who were herding students onto the buses, and then kind of ignored the no-running-in-the-hall rule. We slammed into the office, almost crashing into the counter.

"Election registration is closed," Mrs. Collins told us when we asked for the form. "The deadline was yesterday."

Georgie looked crestfallen. (Which means sad and despairing. I guess it's because when a bird gets depressed, the crest feathers on the top of its head fall down.)

It's amazing how fast your brain can work in an emergency. One instant later I said, "Sure. No problem. It's closed to *adding* candidates, right?"

Mrs. Collins nodded. Just then Mr. Stotts came out of his office. "What's up, kids?"

"It's the sixth-grade elections," I explained. "We'd like a registration form for Georgie. Even though registration officially closed yesterday, we're not really *adding* anyone. We're *subtracting*. Yesterday there were four candidates for president. Lana's out. I'm out. Georgie's in. So now there'll only be three."

Mr. Stotts gave us a long, hard stare. "I see. The two of you are forming a coalition in support of a Sinkoff candidacy, huh?"

Lana nodded. I had no idea what a coalition was, but I nodded anyway. (I looked it up later. Pronounced "koh-ah-LIH-shun," it means an alliance, like Lana and I teaming up for Georgie.)

"Have you ever run for office before, Georgie?" Mr. Stotts asked.

Georgie shook his head.

"Well, you are now. I like this. Put him on the ballot, Francine."

We ignored the no-running rule even faster on the way back to the parking lot. Lana is really speedy. She and I reached Mrs. Wikowitz, who was standing impatiently beside our bus door, at almost the exact same time. (I won by a little.) Lana clambered up the steps with me right behind.

Georgie got on last and yelled to everyone on the bus, "Attention, everyone! My name is Georgie Sinkoff, and I'm running for class president."

Lots of kids cheered. Alex Welch, who was sitting with a bunch of kids from room 111, cheered like Georgie was his bestest best friend. I looked at Eddie Chapple. He looked not happy and also confused. He didn't know Lana and I had dropped out of the race. I bet he was wondering how many kids were going to be running against him.

Then Georgie raised his arms and hollered, "Vote for Georgie Sinkoff!"

Someone started yelling "Sink-off! Sink-off! Sink-off!" and lots of others, me included, joined in.

Georgie was grinning as he sat down. I was grinning, too, until I noticed which seats Oddny had saved. She and Georgie were sitting together. The only empty seat was next to Lana.

One second after I plopped myself down, Alex Welch leaned over the seat back and whispered VERY LOUDLY, "Smoochy smoochy."

It was a one-hour ride to Minute Man National Historical Park.

I don't remember much of the bus trip because I fell asleep.

Minute Man National Historical Park is in Lincoln, Massachusetts, which is near Lexington and Concord. The park is all about the Revolutionary War, which, as you probably learned in school, was filled with stuff like the Declaration of Independence, the Boston Tea Party, lots of battles, and George Washington crossing the Delaware River while standing up in a rowboat (pretty risky, IMO). But to me, one of the most interesting things about the Revolutionary War is Paul Revere's ride.

During our bus trip, Mrs. Wikowitz read us a

famous poem by Henry Wadsworth Longfellow called "Paul Revere's Ride." (Okay, I didn't really fall asleep on the bus. I was just pretending to be asleep so I wouldn't have to listen to Lana chattering about nothing and something and everything else.)

Lots of kids have heard Longfellow's poem. Here's how it begins:

> *Listen, my children, and you shall hear*
> *Of the midnight ride of Paul Revere,*

It has the famous line, *"One, if by land, and two, if by sea,"* and goes on to tell how Paul Revere warned the American colonists "the British are coming!" and how the Revolutionary War began with what later became known as "the shot heard round the world."

That phrase is from another poem Mrs. Wikowitz read called "Concord Hymn" by Ralph Waldo Emerson.

So you might think, *Okay, you listened to some poems. So what?*

Well, here's what.

Mrs. Wikowitz is a different kind of teacher. She

doesn't just read a bunch of poems and tell us history and stuff. She shows us how we have to use our brains to figure things out instead of just believing everything we hear.

For example, despite what Longfellow's poem says, Paul Revere was *not* the only rider who alerted the colonists. There were two other guys hardly anyone has heard of, William Dawes and Samuel Prescott. Right now I'm going to make them famous with my own poem!

Another rider was William Dawes.
He got left out just because.
And if Samuel Prescott had a
rhymable name,
He'd be the one with all the fame.

—CHEESIE MACKSWORTH SHORTFELLOW

When we got to Minute Man National Historical Park, we discovered that many of the park rangers were dressed as Colonial militiamen, British Redcoats, and women in old-fashioned skirts. While we watched, they acted out battles and showed us how the Revolutionary War got started right there. Today history books call it the Battle of Lexington and Concord, but back then it was called the Lexington Alarm.

(Which National Parks have you been to? Go to my website and tell me.)

One of the militiamen let me hold a Revolutionary War musket. It was heavy! Then one of the Redcoats gave us a musket-firing demonstration. It was loud! And there was lots of smoke.

I would've had a terrific time, except Alex kept saying "smoochy smoochy" whenever Lana got near me. He wouldn't stop no matter what I said. It was so annoying that once our picnic lunch was over, I *accidentally* (if you know what I mean) got separated from my group.

When my homeroom walked toward the North Bridge where "the shot heard round the world" was actually fired in 1775, I was sort of *accidentally* out of sight behind a bunch of trees doing some very close scientific examination of some really interesting orange-and-black toadstools. When I looked around, my class and all the other visitors had disappeared. In fact, the only people I could see were dressed in eighteenth-century clothes.

One of the dressed-up women saw me standing alone. "Young soldier, are ye separated from thy brigade? Where be thy commanding officer?"

"I know not," I said, imitating her style of talking. "I must locate the rest of my militia." I pointed toward the North Bridge and trotted away. A minute later I was on the Battle Road Trail. The only soldiers I saw were dressed in red.

"There he is!" a familiar voice yelled. Several Redcoats spun around.

One of my own company had betrayed me.

The Shout Heard Round the World

I, Chester MacRonald, ducked behind a tree.

How had this happened? Only a few minutes before I had been with the rest of the Gloucester militia, preparing to battle the Redcoats. And now I was alone in the silent, sunlit woods, without a clear thought as to which way be safety and which way be capture . . . or worse.

I had been roused to action the night before, many

hours after I had blown out my candle. From deep sleep I was awakened by approaching hoofbeats. *Who would be riding so hard and fast this late at night?*

I leaped to the window just as a man I knew not galloped past, his horse's breath puffing white mist in the moonlight.

"The British are coming! The British are coming!" he yelled for all to hear.

I donned boots and coat, grabbed my musket, powder horn, and leaden balls, and ran out into the night, heading for Robert Louis Stevenson's farm, where our militia had been told to assemble.

And now, in the cool April morn, I had become separated from my compatriots. I cursed myself for stopping to talk with Elaine Shannon, the Post Road rider's daughter. That conversation had delayed me, and now, the Lexington Alarm in full fight, I was surrounded by Redcoats.

"There he is!" a familiar voice shouted.

The Redcoats spun around, muskets raised. I would be made prisoner before firing even a single shot for my country.

One of my own company had betrayed me.

* * *

In a place like Minute Man National Historical Park, with all the monuments and old buildings and costumes, it's easy to imagine yourself back in time. So I wrote the paragraphs above to put you in the mood.

I showed this chapter to Mrs. Wikowitz, and she

told me it is an example of historical fiction, which in one way is harder to write than realistic fiction because you have to get all the historical facts right. For example, I started to use the word *bullets*, but then learned that no one called them that in 1775.

And I know I'm too young to have been a real militiaman, so I pictured Chester MacRonald as being about seventeen (but I read there were boys my age who served as drummers and messengers). I made the character names more realistic by changing Lana Shen to Elaine Shannon (there were no Chinese Americans in New England in 1775) and turning her father (who's a mailman) into a Post Road rider, the mailman of the eighteenth century.

I bet, like me, you've often wondered what it would be like to go back in time. I don't think I would actually want to be in Lexington or Concord with musket balls flying past my head, but it would be cool to have a time machine.

Chapter 10

Georgie's Great Idea

The traitor who ratted me out to Mrs. Wikowitz was (of course) Alex Welch. Georgie told me how it happened:

1. After my homeroom group watched a short video in the visitor center, Mrs. Wikowitz did a roll-call check and discovered I was gone.

2. Georgie tried to cover for me by suggesting that maybe I was in the bathroom, and went to check.

3. But actually he ducked outside to look for me.

4. Alex followed Georgie, saw me, and tattled.

5. I was busted, which was bad because . . .

6. My punishment was I had to sit up front right next to Mrs. Wikowitz on the bus ride home, but it turned out not to be so bad because . . .

7. I didn't have to sit next to Lana and have Alex do his smoochy routine.

On the bus trip, most kids played games on their phones or talked with friends. I would've played a game on my phone, but I was sitting with Mrs. Wikowitz. She handed me her copy of *Treasure Island*, so by the time we got back to Gloucester, I was way ahead on that assignment. (I have always wondered why you can get carsick reading in a car, but no one gets "bussick" reading on a bus. If you have a theory, please go to my website and tell me.)

I guess Georgie's announcing he was running for class president had gotten Eddie thinking about his own campaign because while we were on the field trip he came up with a creative idea. He bought a minuteman picture in the gift shop, taped a petition to it, and passed it around the bus.

It read: *I'm a patriot. I'm going to vote for Eddie Chapple for RLS sixth-grade class president!*

Eddie's petition was actually wrong. We're the RLS Pirates, not the Patriots. But it worked anyway. When the petition got to the front row, I saw that sixteen kids had signed it. I didn't know any of them very well. None had gone to Rocky Neck Elementary School.

That got me thinking about Georgie's campaign. For him to win, he'd have to make himself known to all the sixth graders. We'd need posters and slogans and stuff. And on election day, when the candidates for each office gave speeches to the whole sixth grade, he'd have to do something really special.

As we unloaded from the buses in the school parking lot, I told Georgie, "We've gotta write you a super campaign speech. You know, for the assembly."

"No problem," he replied. "I've got it totally under control. I'm not going to give a speech."

"You have to."

"Nope. I—me, Georgie—don't," he said, grinning widely. "The Great Georgio is going to give my speech."

"THE GREAT GEORGIO!" I screeched. It was so smart, I had to punch him in the arm. The Great Georgio is the name Georgie uses when he does his magic act. He dresses up in an excellent costume, and he's really, really good.

I guess I'd screeched too loudly, because a group of kids, including Eddie Chapple, looked over at us. I immediately shushed myself and whispered, "Don't tell anyone. That is posilutely absitively one of your best Great Ideas."

We were almost at the bicycle rack when I saw Lana waving at me like she always does, except this time she seemed anxious or excited about something.

She and Oddny came running over. "Check out what you're up against, Georgie," Lana said, pointing.

One bus away, a blond girl was moving through a gang of kids, saying hi to everyone.

"That's Diana Mooney," Lana said.

Studying Diana, I could tell right away that she was one of those bouncy girls who are full of energy all the time and always in a good mood. She got to

Knows everyone

Very friendly

Smiles a lot

Full of energy

us while Georgie and I were unlocking our bicycles.

"Hiya, Lana! Hiya, Oddny." Then she turned toward me. She had green eyes and braces. "Hi, I'm Diana Mooney. What's your name?"

"Cheesie."

"Glad t' meet ya, Cheesie," Diana said. "Hiya, Georgie. You're in my math class, right? I hear you're running for president, too. Well, good luck to both of us." She shook Georgie's hand and smiled broadly. "This election is going to be fun!"

She waved a hand-flappy goodbye and bounced away to chat with more kids.

"She's going to win," Georgie said. "She knows everybody."

"Not true," I said quickly. "She didn't know me."

"She does now," Georgie shot back.

"But I've already forgotten who she is," I said. I made a stupid face. "Diana what?"

"We need a petition like Eddie's," Oddny said.

"Or something to hand out to every sixth grader so they won't forget Georgie's name when it's time to vote," Lana said.

"Like what?" Georgie asked.

I jumped in. "My dad has business cards for his limousine service. He hands them out to everyone. I'll ask him where he got them."

"What we really need to do," Oddny suggested, "is come up with ways to make Georgie stand out."

"He already stands out," I joked. "He's the tallest boy in the sixth grade."

"That's it!" Georgie blurted. "I have another Great Idea! Come on, Cheesie. We gotta get to my house." He jumped on his bike and started pedaling.

"Um, goodbye, Lana . . . Oddny . . . see you tomorrow," I said, then hopped on my bike and pedaled super fast to catch up.

On the way home Georgie told me his Great Idea. When we got to his house, he called his dad at work and got permission to use some of the lumber and tools in his basement workshop. I ran home and convinced Granpa to come over and help us with Mr. Sinkoff's table saw. I also called my dad and told him Georgie needed business cards.

"Very smart thinking, Rondo!" Dad said. "I'll phone my buddy at the copy shop and call you back at Georgie's."

Granpa walked over to Georgie's with me. In the basement, Granpa set up the table saw, then waggled his hands at us. "You have to count your fingers before you turn this thing on," he warned. Then, with a lot of buzzing and flying sawdust, he cut the lumber just like we needed. "And then you count them again when you're done." He showed us his hands. "Ten. Close enough. I'm going back to watch the Red Sox."

Right after Granpa left, Dad called.

"You can pick up Georgie's order at the copy shop," he said. Then he mysteriously added, "But it's not business cards."

We pounded some nails and screwed in some

screws, and Georgie's newest Great Idea was finished! (I'm going to keep what we built secret for a few pages. You're going to love it!)

It was almost five o'clock when we hopped on our bikes and rode down to the harbor to pick up Georgie's mysterious not-business-cards.

"It's all paid for," the copy shop guy said. (Thanks, Dad!)

Georgie had brought money from last year's birthday. He put that away and opened the box.

"Stickers!" he shouted. "This is way better than business cards! Everybody loves stickers!"

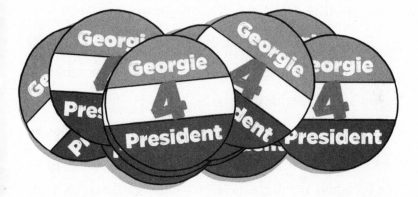

(If you want your own Georgie for President stickers, go to my website.)

"There must be five hundred in this box," I said.

"We can give one to every sixth grader and have enough left over to do it all again!"

That night I ate at Georgie's house. Mr. Sinkoff asked Georgie what he wanted for dinner, and Georgie said, "Breakfast," so we had waffles and bacon. Then we ate strawberry pancakes sloshed with whipped cream for dessert!

Because of the field trip we had no homework, so we decided to make campaign posters.

"I have to feed my dog first," I said.

"No problem," Georgie said. "It'll take me a while to dig the poster-making junk out of my art closet. I'll have it all spread out by the time you get back."

Georgie has a ton of art stuff. He's an excellent cartoonist. He wants to be a movie animator when he grows up. Or a Navy SEAL.

I ran out Georgie's kitchen door toward my house. The sun was almost down, and the sky was purplish as I pushed through the won't-close-gate and into the gully that separates our houses. I rock-hopped across the little creek into my backyard.

My dog—a female springer spaniel named Deeb—

heard me coming before I even opened our back door. I expected her to be jumping all four feet off the ground, which is what she does when she's really hungry, but she just trotted out to me. I rubbed her head and yelled, "Someone feed Deeb already?"

"Yeah, I did!" Goon shouted back from somewhere inside. "I didn't know where you were. I thought you forgot."

"Thanks, Junie!" I yelled back. "I was just over at Georgie's. We're making posters for his campaign."

You probably noticed I didn't call her Goon just then. I guess I was being nice to her because she'd been nice to my dog. But she was wrong. I never forget to feed my dog.

Since I hadn't seen Deeb all day, I wrapped my arms around her and gave her a huge hug. When she was a puppy, those hugs always got me a wet face. Dogs like to lick, and puppy-Deeb *really* liked to lick!

This is not exactly a book on dog training, but I know

something that is really important if you're a kid with a dog and you don't exactly love dog slobber.

Since dogs are natural hunters, they are very observant (excellent sense of smell, good hearing, and pretty good eyesight). So your dog is going to sense everything you do, even if you don't know you're doing it. And since your dog is nowhere near as smart as you are, who do you think would be easier to train? You, or your dog?

You, of course.

So if you have a face-licking dog (or any other bad-habit dog) and you can't get her to stop the licking (or any other bad habit), you're probably giving her some not-so-obvious signals that it's okay for her to slobber all over you (or whatever). Maybe it's the look in your eyes . . . or your posture . . . or the way you talk.

You've developed a bad habit, and you've got to break it.

My bad habit was, even though I didn't like Deeb licking my face, something about it made me laugh. And when I laughed, Deeb got excited and thought she was doing something good. As soon as I figured that out, I trained myself not to laugh or smile whenever Deeb licked me (even if she was really cute when she did it), and that's why I am a dog owner who does not get covered in dog spit.

You should try it. It really works.

After I gave Deeb's head a good, long rub, we wrestled on the grass for a while.

It's weird how sometimes you just know someone is watching you. I looked up to find Goon staring at me from inside the back door.

"What?"

She opened the screen door. "You're working on Georgie's posters?"

"Yeah. Why?"

"I figured this might give you and Georgie some good ideas."

She was holding out the poster she had made for me, which I had taped inside my bedroom door. Leaving Deeb scratching herself on the grass, I got up and took it from her.

"Thanks. But stay out of my room."

It was dark when I ran back through the

won't-close-gate. Deeb stopped at the gate. She will never leave our yard unless I call her. "Come on, Deeb!" I yelled.

She chased after me. We ran into Georgie's house and up to his bedroom.

"Hello, smelly dog," Georgie said.

My dog does smell like a dog. It's no big deal, I'm used to it. I slapped Goon's poster against Georgie's door and pressed the tape down.

Georgie was impressed. "I hate to say it, but your sister does excellent lettering."

"Yeah, maybe," I said. "But we can make posters that are just as good. We'll copy her design and add some of your cartoony stuff."

"Like this?" Georgie asked. He grabbed a new piece of poster board and a black marker. He printed "Georgie" on the poster, but switched to a red marker for the letter *o* and the circle part of the second *g*.

I watched him closely. His tongue sticks out of his mouth when he draws. You can actually tell which way his hand is moving by looking at where his tongue points.

"These two letters will be the lenses of my glasses," Georgie said. "My glasses are kind of like my trademark, and this'll make the posters really special."

I watched as he added the glasses parts that went back to his ears.

"Very cool," I said.

"Yep," Georgie responded.

Over the next hour we made ten posters. We had one or two for every hallway in the school. I did all the lettering except for the red glasses.

"You know what's weird?" I asked when I had finished.

"What?" Georgie replied, barely looking up.

"I'm sure Goon is happy I'm no longer running. But doesn't it seem strange that she would want to help you?"

"Probably she likes me more than you," he mumbled.

I stared at the poster she had made for me. "She likes anyone more than she likes me."

"Forget about her," Georgie said, putting the cap back on his marker. "Tomorrow we are bringing my Great Idea to school!"

Chapter 11

Standing Tall for Sinkoff

I got up early the next morning, dressed super fast, and ran over to Georgie's. Just as I zoomed in their kitchen door (I never have to knock, it's a best-friend thing), I heard Mr. Sinkoff asking Georgie what he wanted to eat, and I guess because we'd eaten breakfast the night before, Georgie said, "Dinner." Mr. Sinkoff grinned at us and made spaghetti and meatballs.

Dee-lish!

Then Georgie called Oddny. "Remember I said I had a Great Idea for my campaign?" he said over the phone. "Here's the deal. Call Lana and meet us in the school parking lot fifteen minutes before the bell. Nope. A surprise. You'll see."

"You know her phone number by heart?" I asked.

"No biggie," he replied. "Science homework help. Remember?"

We couldn't carry the ten rolled-up posters and Georgie's newest Great Idea on our bikes, so Mr. Sinkoff drove us to school. The girls were waiting in the parking lot as requested, so we unloaded, and while Georgie trained them—(I know! You're wondering, *Trained them to do what?* Be patient, I'm getting there!)—I stashed all the posters in my locker, ran to the principal's office, and:

1. Told Mr. Stotts that Georgie's Great Idea was part of our campaign for president.

2. Showed him the note from Mr. Sinkoff giving us permission to use Georgie's Great Idea.

3. Explained that Georgie's Great Idea wasn't actually dangerous at all.

4. Promised we wouldn't let any other kids try it.

It took some convincing, but Mr. Stotts finally agreed. I ran back to the parking lot, and all four of us walked back into the school on Georgie's Great Idea . . . stilts!

Our homemade stilts were an immediate sensation!

"Stand tall for Georgie Sinkoff!" we announced loudly as we clomped down the halls. When a crowd

would gather (every twenty feet!), we'd hop down, hand out Georgie's stickers, and hop back on the stilts again. Every place we went, kids gathered around asking all sorts of questions and begging to try the stilts. But of course we didn't let them. (Thank you, Mr. Stotts!)

Just before the bell rang for first period, we said *See ya later!* to a huge crowd of not-just-sixth-graders and stilted through the kids to Mrs. Wikowitz's classroom. She was standing outside the door, and when all four of us approached clompingly (not a real word, but very descriptive, IMO), I saw what I think was a tiny smile.

After Core, Lana and I walked up the stairs normally, then stilt-walked along the second-floor corridor to our science class.

"Stilts!" shouted Mr. Amato when he saw us. "An excellent demonstration of balance, equilibrium, and center of gravity."

After a couple of physics lessons using stilts, with me as his helper, Mr. Amato led us outside, where he balanced one of my stilts straight up and down on the palm of his hand. It looked really hard to do, but when I got home, I tried . . . and did it. Except with a broomstick. A stilt was too heavy.

The balancing thing is actually pretty easy. I put a description on my website if you want to try it. Just make sure you do it somewhere far from windows and other breakables, because you are sure to crash a few times.

School got even weirder when Lana and I stilt-walked into fourth-period math. Ms. Hammerbord got all giddy and goofy.

"Ooh!" she gushed. "I loved stilts when I was a kid. May I try them?"

"Um . . ." I hesitated. "Mr. Stotts said nobody else—"

"He meant no kids," she said excitedly. "Teachers are exempt from that prohibition."

The entire class went dead silent as Ms. Hammerbord climbed onto my stilts. She teetered for a moment, then laughed and walked back and forth in front of the class. She taught the entire period standing on my stilts. We couldn't take our eyes off her!

"You should teach on stilts all the time," I said when she gave the stilts back to me. "Everyone pays attention!"

We were a big hit everywhere we went. Crowds walked behind us chanting Georgie's name. Lana figured out how to do a half spin on one stilt without falling. Lots of seventh and eighth graders stopped to chat and watch, including Kevin Welch. He said, "You guys deserve to win. This is the coolest gimmick ever. If I could vote, I'd vote for Georgie twice!"

I saw Goon approaching with her so-called boyfriend, Drew, so I leaned down and whispered to Kevin. As Goon walked by, he called out to her, "Hey, Junie! You must be very proud Cheesie's your brother. He and Georgie are the talk of the school."

All the kids surrounding us turned to look at Goon. She blushed. Four points for me! The score was 694–685. (Thanks, Kevin!)

Yesterday I bet there were hundreds of kids who didn't know Georgie Sinkoff. But after today . . . probably none! Georgie's stickers were everywhere! In the history of Robert Louis Stevenson Middle

School, I am sure there has never been a campaign for sixth-grade president this terrific.

Halfway through lunch, however, Mr. Stotts's voice came over the loudspeaker: "Georgie Sinkoff and the other students with stilts . . . please come to my office immediately."

Kids in the cafeteria cheered, booed, laughed, and hooted.

"Uh-oh," Lana said. "Are we in trouble?"

"Only one way to find out," Georgie replied. "Follow me!"

We wooden-legged through the halls toward the school office. Georgie was so fast, by the time the rest of us got there, he was already inside, handing a sticker to the secretary.

"I'd really appreciate your vote and support, Mrs. Collins," Georgie said, sounding just like a politician.

"I will definitely vote for you the next time I am a sixth grader," she replied, smiling warmly.

Mr. Stotts directed us into his office. I was surprised to see Eddie Chapple sitting there. He looked very serious.

"Kids," Mr. Stotts began, "we've got a problem with those stilts."

"I kept my promise," I said quickly. "We didn't let anyone else . . . I mean, Ms. Hammerbord said teachers were allowed to try them."

Mr. Stotts smiled. "That's not it. Your campaign slogan is 'Stand tall for Sinkoff,' right? Well, the problem is, Eddie here says his campaign slogan is 'Rock and roll with Eddie,' and he wants to campaign through school tomorrow on his skateboard."

"That seems fair," Georgie said politely. "I don't mind."

Georgie smiled at Eddie, but Eddie wouldn't even look at him.

Mr. Stotts shook his head. "No skateboards in school. That's the rule. And therefore, from now on, no stilts, either. Leave them here. You can pick them up after school."

"But—" I said.

Mr. Stotts raised a hand. "Nope. Let's move on now. Enjoy the rest of your lunch."

We all walked out into the hallway. Oddny said, "Too bad we had to stop. I was really having fun."

I thought Eddie would be happy about shutting us down, but he scowled and said, "Go ahead. Have your fun. You guys may have won this battle, but we'll see who wins the war after we give our speeches."

He walked away kind of stiff-legged and jagged and proud.

"We did win the battle," I said after Eddie had gone. "Mr. Stotts may have confiscated our stilts, but the Sinkoff legend has been established. Stand tall for Sinkoff!"

Georgie grabbed the girls' hands and held them high. Lana grabbed mine.

"Stand tall for Sinkoff!" we chanted over and over, walking four abreast down the hall, our arms in the air.

As we passed by my locker, I suddenly remembered. "The posters! We forgot to put up Georgie's posters."

Lana raced to get some tape. Then Georgie and I went one way, the girls went the other, and before the end of lunch, we had our posters all over school. We even put one in the boys' PE locker room.

That's where we learned about the sabotage.

As we dressed for sixth-period PE, Glenn said to me and Georgie, "Your presidential campaign posters employ a surprising strategy."

"Thanks," Georgie responded, and went off to the bathroom.

I looked up at the poster. Surprising? What was so surprising about our posters? We had written Georgie's name, the office he was running for, and some adjectives describing him. Nothing about any of that was the least bit surprising. But Glenn is really smart. He doesn't just throw words around.

"What do you mean?" I asked.

"The acrostic."

I had no idea what an acrostic was, and I guess Glenn could see that in my expression. He explained, "An acrostic is a series of written lines in which certain letters, usually the first letter in each line, form a message when read top to bottom."

Then I got it. I'd been tricked. Look at the poster

Georgie

Sinkoff is

Untiring
Good-Natured
Likeable
Your best candidate
for 6th grade president!

and you'll get it, too. Here's an example of an acrostic poem I just made up that reveals who the villain was.

Guess who was the joker.
Only one girl could fake me that bad.
Oh, how I'd like to croak her.
Nobody else could make me so mad.

Coach T blew his whistle, and everyone headed outside. I dawdled at the door, and when Georgie caught up, I told him how we'd been bamboozled. When it was Cheesie for president, Goon had aimed her trickery at me. But now, without knowing what I was doing, I had plopped her deviousness onto Georgie. We had put posters all over school that said Georgie was UGLY.

I was angry. Even worse, I had embarrassed my-self big-time and, according to my Point Battle rules, would have to award my sister eight points. Even worser (there's no such word, but I was really mad!), I had embarrassed my best friend.

"That's bad," Georgie said, staring at the poster on the locker-room wall.

"I know. I'm sorry," I mumbled.

"No," Georgie continued. "It's really bad."

"I know! I'm really sorry."

"No! You don't get it. I mean it's wicked bad! It's so bad, it's good."

"Huh?" Now I was confused.

"The stilts thing?" Georgie said. "All we were trying to do was to get me noticed. Stand tall for Sinkoff! And it worked, right? So if the posters say

I'm ugly, so what? It's something that will stick in kids' minds and help them remember my name. Just like the stilts, it'll get me noticed. And that'll get me more votes."

Georgie suddenly hunched up his shoulders and began swinging his arms like an ape. "People say Ugly Ee-Gorg. Ugly Ee-Gorg happy. Everyone vote Ugly Ee-Gorg to president."

Georgie had turned into Ee-Gorg the monster, so I instantly became Dr. Frank N. Cheez, the mad scientist who had created him. I jumped onto Ee-Gorg's back, grabbed his dim-witted head, shook

it from side to side like a maniac, and whispered fiendishly, "Yes, my monstrous friend! We will tell everyone we did this on purpose. And you, my Ugly Ee-Gorg, will become president. And I—bwa-ha-ha!—will defeat my archenemy . . . Goonzilla!"

Maybe you remember Ee-Gorg and Dr. Cheez from my earlier books. Georgie and I invented them when we were in third grade.

I laughed crazily as Georgie shambled us toward the running track. Lots of boys looked at us, probably wondering why I sounded so insane.

Bwa-ha-ha!

Goon would get no points after all. The Point Battle score remained 694–685.

Chapter 12

Splinter and Splint

After school, we walked all the way home on our stilts. Some people passing in cars honked at us.

Once we got home, I came up with a great game. I challenged Georgie to a stilt-joust in my backyard. We started out far apart, then stilt-ran toward each other as fast as we could. When we met, we tried to shoulder each other over. It was just like knights jousting on horseback, except we weren't carrying lances. (If you think about it, the only way you could hold on to two stilts *and* a lance would be to have three arms!)

"First to win three jousts is the winner," I called out.

Joust #1—As soon as I started moving,
Deeb began barking and then bit
the bottom of my stilt. I fell over
and called Dog Interference. I put
Deeb in the house. No score.

Joust #2—Georgie snagged
a stilt on our sprinkler and
called Lawn Interference.
I moved the hose. No score.

Joust #3—We stilt-ran toward each other at
super speed, but we both tripped and fell
before we met. No score.

Joust #4—We started a little slower this
time, but as we lurched past each other,
our shoulders never touched, and we both
collapsed on the grass. Lots of laughing,
but no score.

Joust #5—This time we each put
on a fierce face, hurtled
forward, smashed into each
other, and fell over. I acted out
an awesome death scene. No score.

We lined up again. That's when Georgie's attempt to trick me led to a disaster.

Joust #6—It started like all the previous
contests, but just before we met, Georgie
dug one stilt into the ground and spun
around on it sort of like the half spin Lana
invented, but way faster. His plan was
to fake me out and then crash into me from
behind. I think it might have worked,
except he lost control, twisted in the air,
and landed on his right side with his hand
under his stilt. I fell down, too.

When I got up, Georgie was sitting and ouching pretty bad. He was holding his right hand and looking at a huge splinter in his thumb. Georgie is really tough, so I knew it must have really hurt because he was repeating "Ow, ow, ow." He kept saying that all the time as we walked inside and showed it to Granpa.

Granpa took a look at the splinter and tried to

make Georgie laugh. "That's a big piece of wood! I'll need a hammer, a pair of pliers, and a blindfold." (He didn't say who was going to wear the blindfold.)

Georgie is definitely a better splinter patient than I am. I'm not afraid of getting shots and stuff from my pediatrician, but I get all ouchy when someone pokes my finger with a needle. In my family it's almost always Granpa on splinter patrol.

Granpa sanitized Georgie's thumb and a needle with about a gallon of antiseptic, then picked up the needle and grasped Georgie's hand.

"Ow!" Georgie yelped.

"I didn't do anything yet," Granpa said testily.

"You're squeezing my finger," Georgie whined.

Granpa gave Georgie a long look. "I barely touched it."

That's when I noticed that Georgie's pointer finger looked fatter than the others. I guess Granpa did, too, because he gently moved it . . . and Georgie jumped.

"Ow!" Georgie said again.

Granpa put the needle down. "You know, kiddo, I think that splinter can wait."

Granpa went to the phone and dialed Georgie's father at work. Two minutes later we were in Granpa's car, and five minutes later we were walking into my pediatrician's office. (Georgie and I go to the same doctor.) Neither Georgie nor I said anything during the car ride.

"What do you think's going to happen?" Georgie asked me while Granpa was talking to the receptionist.

"I think Dr. Paul's going to amputate your finger."

Georgie started to punch me, but stopped when he remembered his hurt finger.

One hour later, after X-rays, splinter removal, and a bright blue splint on Georgie's right hand (yep, his finger was broken), we were back home. Mr. Sinkoff drove up just as we were getting out of Granpa's car. He looked very concerned and asked lots of questions. It took Georgie about five repeats of "I'm okay" and "It doesn't hurt" to convince his father.

"Even so, I'd like you to take it easy tonight," Mr. Sinkoff said.

Georgie shrugged, waved his splinted hand at me, and went home.

The next morning, Granpa drove me and Georgie to school. Georgie was wearing a red wristband just above his blue splint. "My dad made it. I got the idea from your school-color socks. Remember?"

Lots of kids were curious, so Georgie told the story over and over, exaggerating like crazy.

"Me and Cheesie were on those stilts going about a hundred miles an hour. . . ."

He added special effects.

"Ker-bam! Slam! Crunch!"

And gory details.

"Then the doctor came toward me with this huge needle. . . ."

Wherever Georgie went, Oddny, Lana, and I circled around him, handing out more stickers.

"It was totally worth breaking my finger," Georgie said later, waving his blue splint in the air. "This got me almost as much attention as being on the stilts."

Georgie's posters worked, too. Whenever kids

mentioned the UGLY acrostic, Georgie laughed and said, "Good for you. You found my secret code."

Not everything went our way, however. Both Diana and Eddie had pumped up their campaigns. They had posters everywhere. And Diana came to school with about ten ~~thousand~~ million heart-shaped

cookies. She and a bunch of her friends went all over school handing them out to everyone and saying, "I Heart Diana." She even gave a few to Georgie.

"Pretty good cookies," he told me between bites.

Eddie's supporters were working the halls, too. They were everywhere, handing out professional-looking buttons (I bet they cost a lot) with "Get Ready! Here Comes Eddie!" on them. Georgie took one and pinned it on his shirt.

"It's going to be hard to get Bass Rock and Goose Cove kids to vote for Georgie," Lana said.

"I wonder how many other kids are like you," Georgie said to Oddny. "You didn't go to one of Gloucester's elementary schools, but you're voting for me."

"Good question, Georgie," I said. "We've got five minutes before class starts. Let's get the answer. C'mon!"

The four of us walked quickly to the school office.

Mrs. Collins was on the phone, but when she noticed us waiting, she whispered, "What do you need?"

"May we get a list of what schools all the sixth graders came from?" I whispered back.

She kept talking on the phone, simultaneously moving her mouse and clicking a few times. A few seconds later a sheet of paper printed. She handed it to me.

We crowded in close to look at it.

"There are two hundred sixty kids in sixth grade," I said, pointing at the total.

Robert Louis Stevenson Middle School

Sixth Grade

Fifth Grade Attended	Number of Students
Bass Rk Elem Sch	83
Goose Cv Elem Sch	80
Rocky Nk Elem Sch	67
Misc Pvt Sch	15
Home Sch	9
OOD Tfr	6
Total	260

"Oddny is one of these six," Georgie said, his finger on the *OOD Tfr* line, which stood for "Out of District Transfer."

Our principal walked by. "What's up, guys?"

Lana spoke first. "Just election stuff, Mr. Stotts."

"Like what?" he asked.

"Most kids are going to vote for someone they went to school with last year because they know them," I said.

"And Rocky Neck's the smallest of the three elementary schools," Lana added.

"But these guys"—I pointed at the *Misc Pvt Sch*, *Home Sch*, and *OOD Tfr* lines—"didn't go to Bass Rock, Goose Cove, or Rocky Neck. Can we get the names of those thirty kids?"

Mr. Stotts took the sheet of paper, glanced at it and smiled. "Going for the independent voters, huh?"

I smiled back. "Yeah, I guess. Can we?"

"That info isn't confidential, is it, Francine?"

Mrs. Collins shook her head.

"Go for it, kids. I like your thinking." He smiled again, then added, "But you realize . . . if Eddie or Diana asks, we're going to give them the same list."

"That's fair," Georgie said. "But they probably won't because they don't have Oddny to give them the idea."

Oddny blushed.

Mr. Stotts disappeared into his office while Mrs. Collins clicked her mouse a lot.

Before she got too far, I asked, "Um, could you put homerooms on the list, and could we have four copies?" I turned to the others. "If we divide up the list, it's just seven or eight kids each. We're not going to have a lot of time with everything going on."

I was right. At lunch the campaigning got way more intense. While kids were still going through the food line, a bunch of Eddie's supporters began chanting their button slogan over and over. That got Diana's crowd, which seemed more organized (and louder!), to start up an "I Heart Diana!" chant. It was really loud!

I looked over at Coach T, who was on cafeteria duty. I figured he was going to shut everyone up, but he just leaned against the wall, smiled, and watched the noise war.

Livia Grant and Kandy DeLeon tried to get a cheer going for the Sinkoff campaign, but our supporters were just too disorganized. I leaned close to Georgie and spoke right into his ear. "Let 'em yell. It won't matter. When you do the Great Georgio at the speeches tomorrow, Diana and Eddie will be dead meat."

Georgie spun around. He had a weird look on his face. He grabbed my arm and pulled me out of the cafeteria and into the schoolyard. We could still hear the sound of the chanting.

"What's up?" I asked.

"I can't do the Great Georgio." He held up his red-and-blue-splinted right hand.

It took me a second to realize what Georgie meant. There are probably some magicians who can do one-handed tricks, but I guess the Great Georgio isn't one of them.

"No problem," I said. "We'll write a killer speech instead."

He didn't say anything; he just gave me an I-hope-so look.

Georgie's broken finger got him excused from PE that afternoon. Coach T let him hang out with me, Glenn, Eddie, and about ten others while everyone else played touch football.

Coach T was holding a clipboard. "I'd like you boys to consider being on the RLS cross-country team," he said. "Based on how well you did on your mile run, you could be a major part of the squad."

"What are the requirements for participation?" Glenn asked.

"Discipline, dedication, and teamwork," Coach T replied. "It'll be hard work, but incredibly rewarding. You need technique and guts. I can teach technique. You supply guts."

I looked over at Georgie. He was nodding his head

enthusiastically. That nod was telling me, *You can do this, Cheesie!*

Coach T continued, "My seventh and eighth graders have been practicing since August. I need to build my sixth-grade team. You boys could be part of that."

Coach T motioned for Georgie, then handed him the clipboard. "I've got all your names on this list. If you know you want to participate, tell Georgie." He looked at Eddie, then at me. "Chapple and Mack, I've already checked you off. I won't take no for an answer."

Eddie and I glanced at each other. Josh Lunares, one of Eddie's friends and the son of my Spanish teacher, raised his hand. Coach T pointed to him. "How long are the races?" Josh asked.

"They vary, but mostly three-K. Three thousand meters. That's a little less than two miles."

Glenn whispered sort of to himself, "One-point-eight-six miles."

How does he know stuff like that?

"Are there uniforms?" Georgie asked.

"You bet," Coach T responded. "Really sharp ones. Blue with red trim."

Georgie grinned and held up his school-colors splint and wristband. "Go, Stevenson!"

Coach T started jogging toward the track. "Okay, let's head out!"

Everyone followed.

"I've never been on an organized sports team before," Glenn said. "I think I'll really like this."

It turned out Glenn was right. Three weeks after we started practicing, we had our first meet. The RLS sixth graders finished in first place, and Glenn was the hero!

Scoring for XC (short for "cross-country") is different from any other sport I know. After everyone crosses the finish line, you add up the places of the first four finishers on each team, and the team with the lowest number wins.

Confused? It's actually really simple. Here's what happened in our first meet.

The first four finishers of our archrival, Cape Ann Middle School, came in fourth, eleventh, twelfth, and thirteenth. Adding those up $(4 + 11 + 12 + 13)$ gave Cape Ann a score of 40.

Eddie came in fifth. I finished three steps behind him in sixth place. Josh came in ninth. Those three places $(5 + 6 + 9)$ added up to 20. I did a quick calculation in my head. All Glenn had to do was to finish better than twentieth, and RLS would win.

The course went everywhere, with uphills, downhills, and a few sharp turns. The last leg ran right next to the finish line, where Eddie, Josh, and I were waiting and panting. Then it cut across a park and around a stand of oak trees before finally heading back toward us.

When Glenn ran by, heading for the oak trees, he was dragging. He looked like he was almost out of fuel.

Eddie and Josh screamed, "Go, Glenn, go!"

I had been keeping track of the runners. I yelled, "Glenn Philips! If you pass three guys, we win!"

I couldn't believe what happened next. His arms

began pumping harder. His legs sped up, and he passed a kid from Beverly. Then he was mostly out of sight among the oak trees, his red-and-blue uniform flashing between the trunks. When he reappeared, he had passed a boy from Marblehead. On the home stretch, with only fifty yards to go, I shouted, "One more, Glenn!"

Glenn poured it on. I have no idea where he found the energy. On the last stretch, he was moving so fast when he passed the kid from Ipswich, his jet exhaust almost spun the guy around!

That's what is so cool about cross-country. Even though Eddie, Josh, and I all had better times, it was Glenn's nineteenth-place finish that gave us the victory: RLS 39, Cape Ann 40! We lifted him on our shoulders and carried him around. I had never seen him so happy!

That XC meet happened weeks after the sixth-grade speeches and election, but I thought you'd like to know about it.

Oh, and BTW, Lana Shen turned out to be the

absolute fastest runner on the sixth-grade girls XC team. She came in fifth or better in every meet. She even beat me once in practice. Only once, though.

Oh, and second BTW, Georgie attended every one of my meets. That's just what friends do.

Chapter 13

The Disappearing Streamer

Since we hadn't ridden our bikes to school (because of Georgie's finger), and because Granpa had a chauffeur job later that day, Granpa was waiting for us in a limo when school let out. Lots of kids at RLS didn't know my dad owned a limo company, so there were plenty of stares.

As we neared the limo, I heard one kid ask, "Is the president or some kind of movie star at our school?"

Granpa must've heard him because he hopped out of the car and opened the back door like Georgie and I were celebrities. I got in, but Georgie stood by the door for a moment, waving both arms in the air like a

politician. "Thank you!" he cried. "Vote for Georgie Sinkoff!"

Georgie was in a terrific mood when we left school, but when we got home and I said, "Let's get started on your speech," something changed. He got very quiet. We went up to my room. Deeb came in. I closed the door.

"What's the matter?" I asked.

"Nothing."

I didn't think he was telling the truth, but I got started anyway. "Okay, Georgie. How's this for the beginning of your speech? 'My fellow sixth graders, today is a day we will all remember. Today is when you'll vote for the most courageous, most outstanding, most ugly . . .'"

I thought that would make Georgie laugh, but it didn't work.

"What's the matter?" I asked again.

He sat on the edge of my bed. He had a strange look on his face. "I don't know if I can do it."

"Do what?"

"Give a speech."

I spun halfway around in my desk chair and waited for him to continue. I had no idea what was bothering him.

He began petting Deeb, which was weird because he usually stays far away from her because of her smell. Finally he said, "I get nervous in front of people."

"You do not," I said quickly. "You've done the Great Georgio in front of tons of people, and you never get nervous."

Georgie's shoulders got all slumpy. "That's different. That's not me."

"Huh?"

"When I do magic, I'm a different person," he said. "I'm the Great Georgio, not Georgie Sinkoff."

"What's the difference?" I asked. "You're still onstage. You're still the same human being."

"It's not like that," Georgie said. "I'll get nervous. I know it. I can't explain it any better." Georgie flopped over on my bed and buried his head under my pillow.

After a few moments of nobody talking, I took a deep breath and said, "Okay. Don't worry about it. We'll figure something out. We've got plenty of time. Right now, since lots of kids asked us, why don't we write down directions about how we made the stilts and give copies away tomorrow? Kids'll love it. It'll be like bringing stilts to school without the stilts."

Georgie poked his head out from under my pillow and sort of smiled. "That I can do." He was the old Georgie again.

We worked on the stilt plans for a while. Georgie did most of the drawing because—even with a splinted hand!—he's much neater than I am at that kind of stuff. When we were finished, he wrote *Jet Stilts* across the top of the paper and drew a jet plane next to it, his tongue moving as he added exhaust clouds behind the plane.

Then we trotted downstairs to my dad's office and turned on his copy machine. While we waited for it to warm up, we went into the kitchen for a snack. Goon was at the table, writing. She looked up and glared.

I poured two glasses of milk. Then I got a snag of cookies (*snag* is my word for the number of cookies you can grab with one hand) and gave a half snag to Georgie. "I bet if we made stilts we could sell them to kids and make lots of money."

"Too much work," Georgie replied, munching a cookie.

"Yeah," I glurpled into my milk, then set my glass down on the table as far from Goon as possible.

"Get out of here," she muttered. "I'm working on my ballet essay, and you're bothering me."

We ignored her.

"And also," Georgie said, "probably some kid would get a splinter, and we'd get sued."

"Or fall and break a finger," I said.

"Get out," Goon repeated, not looking up from her paper.

"Or break his butt," Georgie said, pushing me butt-first into the refrigerator.

"Oh, pain!" I yelled. "I'm suing you! You made me get a splinter in my butt!"

We laughed hysterically. It wasn't really that funny, but it was a good way to bother my sister.

It worked! Goon screamed "Shuh tup!" so loudly, she gave herself the hiccups. Georgie laughed, and Goon got embarrassed.

Victory! I gave myself two points. The score was 694–687. We left the kitchen with our snacks and made photocopies of our Jet Stilts plan. (The plans are on my website.) Then we went back up to my room.

"Let's work on your speech," I suggested.

Georgie shook his head, so we played board games until it was time to eat. I wasn't worried. We'd think of something.

At dinner that evening, Goon was in a good mood . . . then a foul mood . . . then a fouler mood.

1. Good mood: "Tonight's the dress rehearsal for my dance recital this weekend."

2. Foul mood: "I have tried and tried, but I cannot come up with a good idea for my ballet essay, and it's due tomorrow."

3. Fouler mood: "What? No! I do not want my twerpy little brother to come to my rehearsal. Please, Mom! Can't he stay home by himself?"

But my dad had a limo job. And Granpa had a meeting at some club he belongs to. And even though it was a school night, Georgie was sleeping over at my house because Mr. Sinkoff had a date with Ms. Dinnington, our school nurse, so I couldn't hang out at his house. And my mother was going through a phase where she thought I was still a little boy. (Of course I could stay home by myself. For crying out loud, I was eleven!) So Georgie and I were forced to go to the high school auditorium to watch my sister's ballet rehearsal.

Goon seemed angry on the ride over, but once we arrived at the high school, her mood changed. "Mom, I'm sorry I acted so upset about the boys coming," she said sweetly. "In fact, I'm glad they're here. I want them to sit with you and the other parents and watch the rehearsal."

I was confused for a moment. Then I realized what she was up to. "No way," I said. "We are not going to sit around staring at a flock of tutus flopping across the stage."

Goon acted really sincere. "Please, Mom? It's important for the dancers to have an audience."

"Don't fall for it, Mom," I pleaded. "She's trying to dump an auditorium full of boredom on us."

Goon gave me an evil smile behind Mom's back.

"Besides," I said, "Georgie and I can't watch. We have to write his speech for tomorrow."

That convinced Mom. Once we arrived at the auditorium, Georgie and I found a place to work, the boys' dressing room backstage. We could hear the music coming from the stage and an occasional shrill shout from Goon's teacher, but there was a door we could close for privacy. I sat at a table with a mirror (I guess for putting on makeup) and got ready to write. I could see Georgie in the mirror, pacing around behind me.

"I know you're nervous about tomorrow," I said, "but it has to get done. How about we write just a really short speech?"

Georgie stopped his pacing and looked at me in the mirror. "Okay. One minute long. Maximum."

I smiled at him. "Two minutes."

He nodded.

"Or three."

"Cheesie!"

I thought for a few moments. "We have to come up with a list of reasons why you're the best candidate. Things like responsible, dedicated, confident, reliable, a good listener, enthusia—"

"Wait," Georgie said. "If I'm going to do this— and I don't guarantee I can—whatever I say cannot be so-so-so boring. Everybody will say junk like that. The kids will space out on me."

"Probably right," I mumbled, putting down my pencil.

"It has to be funny," Georgie said. "And it's got to be something that makes kids remember me. Like the stilts."

"Or the stickers," I said.

"Right."

We sat staring absently, thinking. There was a box of safety pins on the table. For costumes, I figured. Sometimes when you're trying to be creative it's good to have something to fiddle with so you can just let your mind wander. I began to construct a safety pin chain.

Finally Georgie said, "How about I make a bunch of campaign promises? Like softer toilet paper in the bathrooms and hot fudge on Fridays."

"But you won't be able to keep those—"

"Nobody will remember what I promised."

"Lame."

More silence. Well, not exactly silence. There was plenty of music coming in from the rehearsal. My safety pin chain now reached the floor.

"Actually, promises are good," I said. "But they've got to be real promises. And you've got to keep every one. You've got to promise *not* to do what you won't do."

"Huh?"

"Like school uniforms."

"We don't wear school uniforms at RLS," Georgie said.

"Exactly," I said. "That's the point. You say, 'I'm Georgie Sinkoff, and I oppose school uniforms.' You say, 'I'm Georgie Sinkoff, and I'm against a shorter lunch period. And when I'm president, I will not support sixth graders having to attend school on Saturdays.' Stuff like that."

"Cool," Georgie said, smiling.

I wrote it all down.

The music from the stage, which had been sort of slowish, suddenly became fast and jolty. That's probably what gave Georgie our next idea.

"And, and, and," he suddenly blurted, "when I get to the boring parts of my speech, I do it as fast as I can. It doesn't matter if people understand what I'm saying. No one cares anyway, and all the other speeches will be way more boringly boring."

He grabbed the paper with my notes.

"I start very slowly, dragging out each syllable. Like this: 'Hi . . . I'm Georg ie Sink off . . .

and I am run ning for sixth-grade class pres i dent. I am . . ."

He took a deep breath and super-zoomed through the list of words I'd written on my pad: "~~Responsible dedicated confident enthusiastic reliable trustworthy confident and blah-blah-blah.~~"

"And balloons," I said. "You walk up to the microphone holding a big bunch of red and blue balloons."

Georgie gave me a questioning look.

"And a pin." I held up one of the safety pins, then stuck it in my shirt pocket. "You pop them to get everyone's attention."

We both laughed. Our brains were full of ideas now. For the next half hour we came up with lots more good stuff and a totally awesome speech. We timed it using the clock on the wall. Two minutes and forty seconds.

Georgie agreed to do it and then asked, "What now?"

"We're done. Let's explore," I said.

We left the speech papers and snuck into the

backstage area, where there were girls moving every which way. Onstage, there were girls twirling and jumping all over the place.

We tiptoed to the very back of the stage, where large pieces of scenery were stored, one of which was a pirate ship.

"Arrrgh," I muttered as we peered out of its port-holes.

"Look," Georgie whispered, pointing to a ladder bolted to the wall.

I followed the ladder up with my eyes. At the top it connected to a platform hung with lights and ropes and all kinds of stuff. The platform stretched from stage right to stage left. (Mom was in lots of plays in college. She told me what everything's called. If you are interested in theater—like me—there's a stage diagram on my website. You can tell me what plays you've been in!)

We skulked to the ladder and started climbing. Georgie and I are both excellent tree climbers, so this was easy for me. With his splinted hand, however, it was sort of hard for Georgie.

"Arrrgh," Georgie muttered.

"Shh," I warned.

As we clambered onto the platform, Goon appeared in the wings directly below us, dressed in a pink bodysuit and holding two long pink ribbon streamers. Goon draped her streamers over the back of a chair behind her and watched the dancers prancing around onstage. I watched them, too. I have to admit they were pretty good.

Georgie tapped me on the arm and whispered, "I have a Great Idea! Gimme that safety pin." He was holding a ball of twine that had been sitting on the platform.

"What?" I asked quietly, handing him the pin from my pocket.

"Watch." He opened the safety pin, tied it to the end of the twine, and lowered it until the open pin was just above Goon's streamers. He lowered it farther and—I couldn't believe it!—hooked one of the streamers. He quickly pulled it up. When the streamer got close, I leaned over and grabbed it.

Goon was so focused on the other dancers, she never

saw! A few seconds later she turned and discovered only one streamer!

She looked around. She looked under the chair, then behind it, then under it again.

She spun around, looking in every direction—except up! Finally she grabbed her remaining streamer and dashed away, probably to the dressing room to look there.

As soon as she was gone, Georgie took the streamer from me, hooked it back on the pin, and lowered it quickly. When it was just above the chair, he jerked the string and the streamer fell off the pin right onto the chair. Georgie is super good at stuff like that. He reeled in the string just before Goon reappeared. She was frantic, but then totally perplexed when she saw her streamer sitting there in plain sight.

The music changed and got really loud, and Goon spun into the center of the stage waving her streamers. Georgie and I laughed so hard we had to roll over and muffle ourselves. Our spy mission had been a complete success!

Chapter 13 ☠

The Goon Squid

Captain Ehab had commanded me to stay in my cabin, but I, with my pet monkey, Jorjee, had come on deck unseen and climbed the mast to the crow's nest. I looked out across the night sea, marveling at the reflections the full moon made on every wave.

Suddenly there was shouting on the deck below.

Days ago, our pirate ship, the *Sink Naught*, had set out from Gloucester Seaport, seeking the treasure we had buried on President Island. But two other pirate vessels, the *Jagged Chapel* and the *Moon of Diana*, also knew of the treasure. The race was on! Had we been overtaken by one of them?

No.

Our problem was not of human creation. A grotesque creature had risen from the depths of the ocean, thrown a hideous arm around our mainmast, and pulled itself onto the deck. I gazed with wonder and horror at the long pink tentacles curling and snatching at anything within reach. I quaked, and Jorjee scurried behind me in terror.

Below us twisted a gigantic monster of the deep, the dreaded goon squid.

* * *

I have always loved pirate movies, and now that we're reading *Treasure Island* for Core class, I have been thinking a lot about what it must've been like to cross the ocean in one of those old sailing ships. I combined that with what Georgie and I did backstage, and added what Goon looked like when she was dancing with those streamers, and wrote that pirate story.

I got a lot of advice and a few big words from Granpa, who has read tons of books about pirates and sailing ships, including *Moby-Dick*, which is a grown-up novel about hunting whales (not treasure).

Granpa told me the captain in *Moby-Dick* is named Ahab, so my mother, whose first name is Edith, became Ehab.

The name of my ship, *Sink Naught* (*naught* means "zero" or "nothing"), came from Georgie Sinkoff's last name. You can probably guess where the names of the other two ships came from. And if you can't figure out why I turned Georgie into a curious monkey, you probably never read books containing the Man with the Yellow Hat when you were younger.

I would love to be an actor in a pirate movie. The ships are cool, and the costumes are awesome!

Chapter 14

Stuffing the Ballot Box

We waited until all the dancers were onstage for the finale, then scurried down the ladder. Mom must've been in a hurry to get home because moments after we slipped back into the boys' dressing room she opened the door and said, "Time to go."

Whew. We'd returned just in time!

"I hope it wasn't too boring for you," Mom said as we rode home.

Goon sat up front. Georgie and I were in the back. "Not at all," I replied. "We had fun. It was interesting."

"Really interesting," Georgie chimed in.

"We especially liked Junie's ribbon dance," I said.

Goon spun around and stared. I could tell she suspected we had something to do with her mysteriously missing-and-reappearing streamer.

"You watched from backstage?" Mom asked.

"Sort of," Georgie said, poking me in the ribs and grinning.

"Sort of more *up*stage," I said with a laugh.

"Mom!" Goon whined. "Tell him to shut up."

"Be nice, Ronald," Mom said, then looked at Goon. "When do you have to mail in your essay for the ballet?"

Goon sounded worried. "It has to be postmarked tomorrow."

We rode in silence for a few blocks, then I said, "Do you want some help with your essay?"

"From you? No way!"

"Your brother is pretty creative, June," Mom said.

"Mom, please! I'll get it done."

* * *

The next morning, Granpa made oatmeal for breakfast. Goon always complains that Granpa's oatmeal is too sticky or too lumpy or too something. But today she ate it without a word. In fact, she was humming between swallows. Next to her on the table was a big brown envelope.

"Is that your essay?" I asked.

"Yep. Finished it last night." She did a little dance in her chair. "My application is done, done, and done!" She took a drink of OJ and actually smiled at me. "And it's really good."

"I hope you win," I said.

She gave me an I-don't-believe-you look, but I was serious. It would be terrific to have her gone for a week during Christmas break.

Goon looked at Granpa. "Would you take this to the post office for me? It has to be postmarked today."

Granpa was reading the newspaper.

"Granpa?" she persisted. "My application has to get mailed today."

He didn't respond.

"Granpa!"

"I heard your screech the first time," he replied without looking up. "I'll take care of it."

My cell phone buzzed. It was Georgie, texting *meet ya*. That's our signal for bike riding.

He was waiting at our usual spot, holding his handlebars with his splinty finger in the air. "I convinced my pop to not worry so much, so he let me ride to school."

"Today's your big day," I said cheerily. "Speeches this afternoon—and you're gonna be great! Then the vote—and you're gonna win!"

Georgie didn't talk much on the ride to school. I guess he was thinking about his speech. While we were locking our bikes to the school rack, some kid we didn't recognize yelled, "I'm voting for you!" Georgie waved, but he didn't seem very enthusiastic.

As we walked by the school office, a woman's voice called out, "Okay, Georgie. I heard about your hand. Let me see it."

It was Ms. Dinnington, our school nurse. Everyone likes her, especially Georgie's father, who's been going out with her for almost a year. Ms. Dinnington is tall and blond, and Georgie told me she's got a daughter in high school or something.

Georgie held out his splinted hand. "It doesn't hurt. The doctor says I'm fine."

"I just want to see how he treated it," Ms. Dinnington said, taking Georgie's wrist and gently turning it. "Nice job." She let go of his hand and put her hands on her hips. "I hear you're running for class president."

Georgie seemed kind of embarrassed. "Uh-huh."

"Mr. Stotts asked me to stay after school today and count the votes," Ms. Dinnington said. She looked around, then leaned closer. "I'm going to make certain you win. Get it?" She glanced at me, and then gave Georgie a secret wink. It was a lot like a Mack Family squinty-evil-eye.

I was stunned.

Sometimes I'm amazed at how fast the human brain works. In less time than it took me to type the first word in this sentence, this is what went through my mind:

> 1. An official, grown-up, professional school nurse just told us she is going to rig the election in Georgie's favor!

2. Miscounting votes is cheating, and I hate cheating because you never know how good you are if you cheat.

3. Stuffing the ballot box has to be against school rules. If anyone finds out, she'll be fired.

4. I think it's against the law, too. Ms. Dinnington will go to jail, and probably Georgie . . . and maybe me!

5. Deeb. What about Deeb? If I go to prison, will I be allowed to have my dog with me?

I looked at Georgie. I couldn't tell if he was upset or not. He was just staring at Ms. Dinnington. Not blinking. Just staring.

I looked at Ms. Dinnington. Her face was expressionless, too.

Suddenly Georgie burst out laughing, and a microsecond later Ms. Dinnington laughed so hard she snorted. She touched Georgie's shoulder. "I'm very proud of you, Georgie. Good luck today." She went back into the school office.

"What-the-what was all that about?" I asked as we walked down the hall toward homeroom.

"She is the funniest lady ever," Georgie replied.

I was completely bewildered. "What about the votes? Counting? You know . . ."

"It was a joke, Cheesie," Georgie said. "You've never been over at my house when she has dinner with us. Oh my gosh! My dad and I laugh our heads off. She is the funniest lady ever."

Wow! And here I thought she was just the school nurse.

"Is she going to be your stepmom?" I asked.

Georgie didn't answer right away. Then he said, "I don't know."

I thought about how Georgie's mother had died when he was two. It's always been just him, his dad, and his older brothers, all of whom are now grown and out of the house. Finally I said, "I wonder if it's weird to have a stepmom."

"I hope not," Georgie said. "I think it'd be cool to have a stepmom."

In the corridor where all the sixth-grade homerooms are, the walls were covered with posters. So far in this story I've only talked about the contest for class president, but there were also races for vice president, secretary, treasurer, and spirit captain. You can probably imagine the hubbub in the halls (lots of "Vote for me" hub and "I am so cool" bub).

"Oh, no!" I said as we neared Mrs. Wikowitz's classroom. There, on the wall opposite her door, was

Georgie
Sinkoff is
Untiring
Good-Natured
Likeable
Your best candidate
for 6th grade president!

one of Georgie's posters. Someone had "decorated" it with a purple marker—a big nose and a bushy mustache had been drawn under the Georgie glasses.

I handed Georgie my backpack. "Put this on my desk! I'll be right back."

I scooted down the hall as fast as I could without getting busted for running. I turned into the next corridor, and just as I suspected, the purple nose and mustache were on the poster we'd taped to that wall. I spun around and zoomed toward the cafeteria. Yep. There was another nose and mustache on that poster, too. I raced back to class.

Lana, Oddny, and Georgie were waiting near Lana's desk.

Lana grabbed my arm. "What's going on?"

I told them. Lana reached into her SuperBinder and pulled out a purple marker. "It could've been anyone. Lots of kids have these."

The bell rang, and we slid into our seats. Mrs. Wikowitz was staring at me, so I opened my SuperBinder, took out my homework, and held it up for her to see. When she looked away, I turned to Eddie (remember, he sits right next to me in Core) and whispered, "Did you mess with Georgie's posters?"

"Nah," he whispered back, his lips barely moving. "I saw it, but I didn't do it. Don't need to. I'll win anyway."

Eddie had his speech on his desk. When he saw me glance at it, he quickly put it away.

If Eddie wasn't the culprit—and I figured he was telling the truth—then maybe it was Diana. But she didn't seem like the type of person who would vandalize someone else's posters.

I was still thinking about it when Mrs. Wikowitz dimmed the lights. Today we were doing social studies during first period, and since we were still studying prehistoric humans, she showed us a video about some guy who'd been shot with an arrow and frozen in ice for five thousand years. In 1991, some hikers found his body. He'd been so well preserved in the ice, the scientists who studied him could tell what he'd eaten as his last meal!

(I ended up writing a report about Ötzi the Iceman. It's on my website. I was allowed to use it for both science and social studies. Granpa said, "That's top-noodle thinking! Work once, win twice.")

Just before class ended, Mrs. Wikowitz spoke about the election.

"This afternoon during the fifth-period assembly, you'll hear speeches from each of the candidates running for class office. I expect you to take this seriously. It is an excellent opportunity to participate in democracy. Voting is one of the hallmarks of a free society. Cast your votes wisely."

In the hallway after Core, I pulled Georgie, Lana, and Oddny to the side. "Who's got the balloons?" I asked.

"Here," Lana replied, handing me a plastic bag. "They've got 'Happy Birthday' on them. Sorry. They were the only red and blue balloons I could find."

"Doesn't matter," I said, stuffing them in my pocket. "Georgie's going to pop them anyway. I'll pump 'em up with Mr. Amato's helium and stash 'em in the science supply closet until fifth period. Right now, we each have an assignment."

I handed out copies of the list the secretary had printed for us of the thirty kids who hadn't gone to Goose Cove, Rocky Neck, or Bass Rock.

"Check off the names of anybody on this list who's in one of your next classes. We've got to convince them to vote for Georgie."

Between us, we checked off all but four kids.

"Here are some more Georgie for President stickers," Oddny said, passing them around.

"Okay," I said. "Talk to everyone we've checked and make sure to give them a sticker before fifth period."

This was going to be our last chance to campaign. Voting would take place during sixth period. After school, the teachers would take the ballots to the office, where Mrs. Collins and Mr. Stotts—not Ms. Dinnington!—would count them. The results would be announced the next morning.

The girls sped away.

"One last thing," I said to Georgie. "Have you

practiced your speech? Eddie was looking at his before Core."

"Uh-huh." Georgie didn't seem very enthusiastic.

"And you've got the pin to pop the balloons?"

Georgie patted his shirt pocket. He was definitely not very enthusiastic.

"What's going on with you?" I asked.

"Nothing. I mean . . . I don't know. It's just . . ."

I grabbed him by both shoulders. "Georgie, you're making a big thing out of nothing. You're still the Great Georgio. Just do the speech like we planned, and you'll get elected sixth-grade class president! You'll see."

"Okay," Georgie said. "See you at lunch." He walked toward his third-period class. His posture looked slumpy again. He did not seem like my regular Georgie.

Six of the "independent" kids were in my third- and fourth-period science and math classes, so I cornered them one at a time and gave them Georgie for President stickers along with a really short, really enthusiastic pep talk. I guess being singled out made them feel special, because five kids really listened, and I think I convinced them to Stand Tall for Sinkoff.

I invited the sixth guy to help me blow up the balloons after lunch, which I thought would make him want to be a Sinkoff supporter, but while we were carrying the balloons to the auditorium for the speech assembly, he told me he lives really close to Eddie and they're good friends.

You can't win them all! Even so, if Lana, Oddny, and Georgie had done as well with their "independents," we'd picked up a bunch of votes.

Because of the balloons, I was one of the last to get to the auditorium. I dashed around the side and went in the backstage door and looked around. The curtain was still closed. Mrs. Wikowitz was onstage, showing the custodian where to put the lectern and microphone. I could hear the yammer-yammer of all the sixth graders in the audience.

There were about twenty kids backstage, all running for class offices. One of the other sixth-grade homeroom teachers was telling them to sit on a bunch of chairs set up in the wings. That's where I found Georgie.

"Here're your balloons," I said. I tied the strings around his wrist. "This way it'll be easy for you to pop them with the pin."

Georgie wasn't paying attention. His face was white. "Cheesie," he whispered hoarsely, "I can't do this. I'm freaking out."

I had to do something. I pulled him over to the side of the main curtain and opened it just enough for us to peek out at the crowd.

Counting all the sixth graders and teachers, there were nearly three hundred people sitting near the front of the RLS auditorium. It's a pretty big auditorium. Even with that many people in the room, less than half the seats were filled.

"Come on, Georgie," I said. "You know lots of these kids. Maybe even half. And lots are your friends. There's nothing to freak out about."

That seemed to calm him down a little. We went back to the chairs. I didn't know if I was supposed to be backstage, but I figured, since Georgie was acting weird, I had a good excuse. So I sat next to him.

The curtain opened, the audience cheered, and Mrs. Wikowitz introduced the first of the candidates running for class secretary.

We had a long time to wait. The kids running for president were scheduled to speak last. And they were in alphabetical order, so Georgie's would be the very last speech.

I can't remember all the speeches (and even if I did, you wouldn't want me to write about them, because most of them were borrrr-ring!), but here are the highlights:

1. One girl, running for spirit captain, did a cheer, threw some pom-poms in the air, and ended with a split. (I figured that's what spirit captains need to know, so I voted for her later.)

2. A guy came out, screamed "Hi!" into the microphone, said "Vote for me," and walked off. He forgot to say his name or what office he was running for. The audience loved it, but since I didn't know his name, I bet lots of other kids didn't either. (I can't be positive, but I'm pretty sure I didn't vote for him.)

3. Kandy DeLeon ended her speech for vice president by yelling "Vote for Kandy!" That was the signal for Lana, Oddny, and two other friends in the audience to stand and fling handfuls of candy in every direction. The crowd went wild! (Very clever, IMO. I voted for Kandy.)

4. Livia Grant was running for

treasurer. She said, "I will take care of our class's money. And if anyone tries to steal it, my attack dog will get them." Livia then waved "come on" to the side, and two girls pushed a huge cardboard box—the kind refrigerators come in—onto the stage. As Livia picked up the thick rope that hung out of the box, a loud roar came out of the sound system. Livia pulled the rope, and the tiniest dog trotted out.

(Livia's okay, and I really like dogs. I voted for her.)

Finally we got to the speeches for president.

"You're third," I whispered to Georgie. I know he heard me, but he didn't do or say anything.

Eddie Chapple was first. He walked slowly across the stage to the lectern, nodding to his friends and waving. He acted very confident.

"I am a leader," he began. "I believe a leader is someone who is not afraid to do what he thinks is right."

I was listening, but I was looking at Georgie. His lips were pressed tightly together, and he was breathing way too hard for someone who had been sitting in one place for thirty minutes.

Eddie gave a very good speech. He used lots of positive words like *strength, determination*, and *confidence*. The audience interrupted him several times to cheer. As Eddie neared the end of his talk, four boys came onstage, two on each side of him. They were wearing RLS T-shirts. Eddie raised his hands and shouted, "I know every kid who attended Bass Rock with me last year is with me now. And as for the rest of you, if you want the best president, here's who to vote for."

That's when all five guys surprised everybody by pulling off their shirts. Their chests were painted bright blue, with big red letters spelling out E-D-D-I-E. The audience screamed and applauded.

Diana Mooney was introduced next. She sort of

ran onto the stage, waving to everyone. She passed right by the lectern, waved to everyone on that side of the audience, and then came back to the center.

Two girls standing in the wings on the far side of the stage let out a rope that lowered a giant cardboard crescent moon. The moon was painted blue and had red letters that spelled out MOONEY. I looked at the red and blue balloons floating above Georgie's head. We weren't the least bit unique. Everyone was working the school-colors idea.

Then I looked at Georgie. He was sweaty, his eyebrows were waggling up and down, and he was breathing real fast . . . hyperventilating. When I was little, sometimes I'd cry and get so worked up I couldn't stop. Georgie wasn't crying, but his breathing was definitely out of control.

"You can do this, Georgie," I said. "Take a slow breath."

He tried, but he couldn't do it.

"Take a breath through your nose, make your mouth into a small circle, and blow it out real slow."

This is a trick Granpa showed me when I was

little. It calms your breathing. Georgie looked around quickly. No one was paying any attention to us.

"Georgie, trust me. This really works."

He drew in a breath, his chest quaking with anxiety. He pursed his lips and blew out. I could tell he was trying to go slowly and evenly, but his air puffed out in short bursts.

"One more," I urged.

He did it again. This time his exhale was steadier.

"And again . . . slowly," I said.

I was so focused on Georgie, I only caught bits of Diana's speech. She sounded super happy and upbeat. I heard the word *fun* three or four times.

After a few more exhales, Georgie's breathing was almost normal. Then he said, "I'm not doing this speech, Cheesie. I can't."

"It's okay," I said.

"I just can't." Georgie slumped in his chair.

Diana was finishing. She was saying, "So maybe Eddie thinks guys from Bass Rock will vote for him. Well, I'm counting on my Goose Cove friends."

She pointed up at her red-and-blue crescent moon.

"With your vote we can take the sixth grade to the moon! Vote for Diana Mooney!"

A bunch of kids in the audience began yelling over and over, "Goose Cove for Mooney!" Then some of Eddie Chapple's supporters began screaming, "Bass Rock for Eddie!" It was really loud. Diana just stood there, smiling broadly and waving happily to everyone like she was the Queen of Gloucester. Finally the chants died down, and she walked offstage.

"Good luck, Georgie," she said as she passed by.

Georgie was in a daze. He didn't respond.

Mrs. Wikowitz introduced Georgie, and someone in the audience started yelling his name. In seconds, it was a booming chant: "Georgie! Georgie! Georgie!"

Georgie looked straight at me.

Sometimes you have to know when enough is enough. Georgie is my best friend. I count on him, and he counts on me. If he couldn't do it, I knew what I had to do.

"Okay. You don't have to give the speech," I said. "But we've worked too hard to give up. I'm going to give your speech."

Georgie stuck out the arm with the balloons. "Here, take these."

I shook my head and walked to the center of the stage.

Chapter 15

Don't Vote for Georgie!

I measured the distance afterward. It was only thirteen steps from the wings to center stage. But in my memory, it took forever to walk that far.

I was carrying the speech Georgie and I had written, and I guess I was planning to make up some lame excuse why it was me and not him giving it. When I got to the microphone, I placed the speech on the lectern and stared out at the audience.

The "Georgie" chant stopped.

There was silence.

Someone coughed.

I looked from one side of the room to the other. Everyone was staring back at me. I looked down at the speech. It began, "My fellow sixth graders, today is a day we will all remember. Today is when you'll vote for the most courageous, most outstanding . . ."

I could have read that, but I didn't.

Instead I took a deep breath and just spoke, not having the slightest idea what was going to come out of my mouth.

"My name is Ronald Mack. Some of you know me. I'm Cheesie. I mean, I'm not actually cheesy. That means something kind of crummy. That's not what I am. I'm Cheesie. That's my nickname."

I took a deep breath. I wasn't sure I was making any sense.

"Georgie Sinkoff is running for class president. Maybe you're wondering why I'm standing here and not him. Good question."

It was a good question, and I didn't have a good answer. I just stood there looking dumb until my awkward pause was interrupted by some boy yelling "Bass Rock for Eddie!" followed by a girl yelling "Goose Cove for Mooney!" Then Glenn Philips surprised everyone who knew him by standing up, waving his arms, and screaming "Rocky Neck for Georgie!" That got everyone shouting.

Coach T, Mrs. Wikowitz, and a couple of other teachers in the audience moved like they were going to take charge, but they stopped when I raised my arms, leaned close to the microphone, and said slowly and loudly, "May I speak, please?"

I kept repeating that, and the room quieted down. All that screaming had given me an idea. I lowered my arms.

"I've known Georgie Sinkoff my whole life. Like I said, he's running for class president, and I'm his campaign manager. Georgie and I went to Rocky Neck Elementary. We went to that school every year from kindergarten to fifth grade. We had fun there. We'll never forget that. Yay, Rocky Neck!"

Some of my friends started to cheer, but I raised my hand and it stopped.

"Diana Mooney went to Goose Cove. And just like me and Georgie, I bet she had fun there. And I bet she'll never forget that. So I say yay, Goose Cove!"

A couple of kids shouted, "Goose! Goose!" But that

died down fast. I glanced into the wings. Diana was standing next to Eddie.

"And Eddie Chapple went to Bass Rock," I went on. "I'm sure he liked his school, too. Yay, Bass Rock!"

The audience was silent. Everyone was totally paying attention now.

"But that was then. This is now. This is Robert Louis Stevenson Middle School. This is RLS. And that's why I say to all of you . . . DON'T VOTE FOR GEORGIE SINKOFF!"

The crowd went nuts.

I heard, "What? Huh?" And all sorts of hoots and shouts. Everyone was confused. What kind of a campaign speech tells you *not* to vote for someone? I glanced over at Georgie. He was standing now, balloons above his head, his mouth hanging open. I gave him a big thumbs-up, grinned, and turned back to the audience.

"That's right. Don't vote for Georgie. And I'm telling you"—I was yelling now—"don't vote for Eddie or Diana, either! Don't vote for someone just because you went to some elementary school with them! We're all at Robert Louis Stevenson now. Vote for the candidate you think will be . . ."

I held up one finger. "The number one . . ."

I waved both arms in the air. "Most spectacular . . ."

I grabbed the microphone off the lectern and began running around the stage. "Best sixth-grade president in the history of ever!"

Everyone was screaming and clapping. Georgie surprised me by running onto the stage, grabbing the microphone, and yelling, "I'm Georgie Sinkoff, and I approve this message!" He then popped the balloons with the safety pin, tucked me under one arm with his good hand, and carried me offstage.

The applause was tremendonormous!

When we got offstage, the two of us were laughing so hard, we fell down. Mrs. Wikowitz pulled me to my feet. I couldn't believe it. She was grinning!

It was the best election assembly in the history of ever!

As we walked to PE, the whole school was buzzing. Lots of kids came up to me with high fives and back

pats. We got stopped so much, we barely made it to the gym in time. While we changed clothes, Coach T gave us each a ballot and a little pencil. I voted (for Georgie, of course!) and put my ballot in a box on Coach T's desk.

Eddie was right behind me. He dropped in his ballot. "Very sharp speech, Cheesie." His face, which is normally thin, seemed pinched and nervous. "I thought I had this, but now, I gotta admit, I think Georgie's got a real chance."

Everyone else in PE played volleyball, but I convinced Coach T to let me run around the track because I was so revved up. I just flew! Coach T said I clocked my best time yet.

After school we were unlocking our bikes and Georgie was asking if he could use my bike pump when we got home because his front tire felt a little squishy, when Oddny and Lana ran up.

"Oh my gosh, Cheesie," Lana squealed. "Everyone is talking about your speech!"

"Georgie's going to win!" Oddny blurted. "We have to celebrate. Frozen yogurt! My mom's driving me and Lana." She pointed to a waiting car. "Meet us there, okay?"

Georgie is cuckoo for frozen yogurt, so before I could say anything, he yippeed, and we were bicycling after Oddny's mom's car.

We coasted down the hill into town, passing bunches of middle school walkers, lots of whom waved or shouted greetings. Running for class president seemed like an excellent way to become popular.

"Do you think I'll win?" Georgie asked me.

"I don't know," I replied. "But I bet it'll be close."

There was no bike rack at the yogurt place, so we locked our bikes together and went in. Minutes later we were at a table with the girls eating our treats. (Thanks, Oddny's mom!) Nobody said much for the first five or six spoonfuls.

"You know," Georgie finally announced between big, drippy bites, "I was actually ready to give my speech. All that nervousness was a fake-out. I was trying to psych the opposition. Cheesie messed me up, taking over like that."

"Liar," I said, bonking his elbow just as he lifted his spoon to his mouth.

The spoon hit his nose and a piece of strawberry stuck there. Everybody laughed, so Georgie left it there on purpose, and we all went back to yumming 'gurt.

(I just checked online, and I think I invented a new phrase! If you prefer ice cream, you can say, "Yumming 'scream.")

"I bet you lose by one vote," I said.

"Why do you say that?" Lana asked.

"Because I voted for Eddie," I replied with a big smile.

Georgie lifted his hand. I expected him to grab me or punch me, but all he did was flick the piece of strawberry off his nose. It missed me.

"Actually, it was totally weird how I freaked out," he said seriously. "I just lost it."

"Everybody freaks out sometime," Oddny said with a smile.

Then we all yummed 'gurt until Lana said to me, "You saved the day for Georgie."

It was embarrassing for her to say that. Georgie's my friend, and that's what friends do.

The four of us sat and talked for a long time, first about RLS and then about China. Lana has grand-parents in Beijing, which is the capital. Then we talked about Iceland. Oddny told us people there don't have last names like we do.

"My brother is Halldor Thorsson," she said. "Get it? Thor's son because Thor is my father's name. And I'm Oddny Thorsdottir. And my father is Thor Baldursson because my grandfather's name was Baldur."

"Cool," I said. "I'd be Ronald Caldwellsson."

"I'd be George Davidsson," Georgie said.

"My dad's name is Donald, but his real name—his Chinese name—is Quon, so I'd be Lana Quonsdottir."

"In Iceland the telephone books list everyone by first names and occupations," Oddny explained. "And everyone calls each other by first names. People even call the prime minister by her first name."

Georgie raised his spoon. "After I'm elected, I will let everyone call me President Georgie!"

Oddny then told us Iceland is so close to the

North Pole it never gets dark in the summer, and kids sometimes play outside games after midnight.

"And in the winter, it's just the opposite. There's no daylight. The sky will start to look a little like sunrise, but then it just gets dark again. My parents say that makes it easier for kids to be good students because it's too dark to play outside."

"You *are* kind of smart," Georgie said. He was leaning way back in his chair because he was really full from eating his huge treat.

"But," I asked, "are you smart because you study? Or do you study because you're smart?"

"Maybe both," Oddny replied with a small smile.

I have to admit it was fun hanging with the girls.

But Lana is not my girlfriend.

Chapter 16

Running for Goon!

When it was time to go, we walked outside and discovered that someone had knocked our bikes over, which was bad because they were locked together. My pedals got stuck in Georgie's spokes and vice versa. It took us a while to unstuck them, and the girls sort of giggled at how clumsy we were. But it was okay because the entire day had been unusual, exciting, and fun, and we were full of yogurt and really happy.

It was after four when we got to Georgie's house. We carried our backpacks up to his room and did our homework (it was easy), then walked through our backyards to get my bike pump for Georgie's squishy tire. I used the hidden key to get in my backdoor, trotted through the house and into the garage, and took the pump off its wall hanger. (Granpa keeps a very orderly garage.) When I got back to the kitchen, Georgie was pointing at the table.

"Look at that! Purple marker."

On the table, just where she had left it, was Goon's envelope with her essay for the ballet in Boston. I hadn't noticed at breakfast . . . Goon had written the address with a purple marker!

"Your sister! She messed up my posters!" Georgie said.

I could visualize the purple nose and mustache on each poster. The purple writing on Goon's envelope wasn't exactly proof (like Lana said, lots of people have purple markers), but I was pretty sure Georgie was right.

"This is more messed up than you realize, Georgie." I picked up the envelope. "This is Goon's application to that Boston dance thing. It has to get to the post office today, and Granpa forgot to mail it!"

"Serves her right."

"Yeah, maybe," I replied. "But c'mon! We have to hurry."

I stuffed the envelope inside my shirt and ran full-speed through our backyards and around Georgie's house to where we'd left our bikes.

"Where are we going?" Georgie yelled to me as we jumped on and pedaled.

"The post office. I really want her to win!" I yelled back.

It was way more than a mile. We should've pumped up Georgie's tire; it was too soft to go full speed.

And we hit every red light.

And I'd left my cell phone in my backpack at home, so I didn't know what time it was. I didn't even know what time the post office closed.

Finally we were on Prospect Street, only a few blocks from the post office, racing downhill. We shot right past a group of girls.

Georgie shouted to me, "That was your sister!"

"I know! I saw her! We've got to get this post-marked!"

We turned onto Dale Avenue, did a crash stop in front of the post office, and ran inside.

No luck.

I read the sign and looked at the clock on the wall: 5:25. The window had closed at 5:00. I ran over to the mail slot. Maybe there was still time. Nope. The last mail went out at 5:00 as well. And there was no postage on Goon's envelope anyway, so even if . . .

Never mind. Goon was doomed.

I leaned against the wall and slid down until my butt was on the floor. Georgie sat down next to me.

"What do we do now?" he asked.

I shrugged. "She's a really good dancer. She could've won. And I would've won because she'd have been gone for a whole week."

We sat, catching our breath.

"Too bad we can't just postmark it ourselves," Georgie said. "You know, write the time and date on it, and then drop it in the slot there. Too bad it has to be officially stamped by someone who works here."

Georgie had just given me an idea. "I know what to do!" I said. "C'mon!" I pulled Georgie up, and we ran outside.

Our bicycles were gone!

"Stay here!" I said to Georgie. "Look for our bikes. I'll meet you back home. I'm running to Lana's."

"Why?" he shouted after me as I ran away.

"Her father's a postman!"

I sprinted a few blocks without thinking about what I was doing. I just ran, Goon's big envelope flapping against my belly with each swing of my arms. I ran past stores and houses. The pavement was still warm from the bright fall sun, but the air was starting to cool. I ran down to the harbor, the caws of the gulls getting louder, and then along the road where lots of lobstermen bring their catch. I smelled the ocean and fish, and I liked it. I ran and ran, my sprinting slowing to an easy sort of floating, my feet barely touching the ground.

Had I been running for five minutes or five hours? It was automatic. It was magical.

Then, as I started up the long hill toward Lana's house, a switch flipped somewhere in my brain, and my mind was filled with nothing but questions:

1. If the post office was closed, what was the hurry?

2. Who could run farther without stopping, me or Deeb? She's faster, but would she poop out before I did?

3. If I get Goon's letter mailed in time and she wins that ballet thing, do I give myself points in the Point Battle?

4. Most cars are white, black, gray, blue, or red. Why are there almost no orange cars?

I have no idea where my ideas come from.

I turned onto Lana's street, and suddenly I was

exhausted. Her house had to be more than three miles from the post office. It took every remaining bit of energy and willpower for me to run (well, actually, I was probably moving at a slow trot) past the last few houses. Lana was on her porch, waving to Oddny, who was just getting into her mom's car. I staggered up, breathing so hard I couldn't talk.

"Your dad," I finally panted out. "I need to talk to your dad."

"What about?" Lana asked. She looked concerned.

"Post office" was all I could say. Then I plopped down on her porch steps.

Moments later Mr. Shen was sitting next to me, listening and watching as I told him about Goon's ballet and pointed to the envelope.

"Is there anything you could—"

"Maybe," he said. "Let's figure this out."

"I want to see what happens," Oddny said. She turned to her mom. "Can I stay? Please?"

"I'll bring her home," Mr. Shen said. Oddny's mom waved and drove off. Mr. Shen led me into the house, where Mrs. Shen gave me something to drink. My breath finally returned to normal. Then Mr. Shen sat at his computer, asked a few questions about Goon's ballet thing, and did a bit of online searching.

"Looks okay," he finally said. "Let's go to the post office."

"Can we come?" Lana said.

A few minutes later we were getting out of the car in the parking lot behind the post office. Mr. Shen unlocked a rear door, and we went into the post office's back room. I expected it to be deserted, but there were several workers sorting and moving letters and packages into slots and bins and carts.

"Whatcha doin' back, Donny?" one of them asked Mr. Shen.

"A special letter," he said, holding up Goon's application.

It was strange to be on the other side of the windows where customers bring their mail. Mr. Shen placed the envelope on the scale, then took money out of his pocket.

"You can pay me back tomorrow," he said with a smile. "When I checked the ballet company website,

it said postmarked today, so this is okay. If it had said by five o'clock today, I couldn't do it." He touched a computer screen a few times and a sticker with the postage and date came out of a slot. He slapped it onto the envelope.

"Let's be double sure," Mr. Shen said, picking up a rubber stamp and smacking it against the envelope. He pointed to where he had inked today's date above Goon's purple address, and then flung the envelope across the room into a basket. We all laughed.

When Mr. Shen dropped me off at home, Georgie was waiting out front, astride his bike. Mine was lying on the lawn next to him. Lana and Oddny shouted goodbyes as Mr. Shen drove away.

"Where'd you find our bikes?" I asked Georgie.

"They were right here," he said. "Weird, huh?"

I was unsurprised. I'd been thinking about the bike-napping on the drive home. "Actually, not so weird," I said. "I bet it was Goon and her friends. She took them just to torture us. Now it's our turn to get her. Din?" I asked.

We eat over at each other's houses so often, we don't even have to ask the whole question. Georgie nodded enthusiastically.

I cornered Granpa while we washed up and told him how he'd forgotten the envelope and what we'd done with it.

"Holy tamales," he whispered. "I owe you a big one."

The second we sat down to eat, Goon turned to Granpa and asked, "Did you mail my application?"

"You don't see it on the table, do you?" he responded sweetly. "Must've gotten taken care of, huh?"

Granpa wasn't exactly lying.

Georgie did most of the storytelling while we ate. He went through the whole day, and when he described the kids' reaction to my speech he made it sound like the auditorium's windows had been blown out by the cheering. The way he told it, I was the Huge Hero of the World.

"That was a wonderful thing to do," Mom said.

"Darn clever!" Granpa said loudly. "Exactly what I'd've done."

Dad gave me a squinty-evil-eye.

Goon looked bored.

Granpa patted Georgie's shoulder. "You're going to win this one, kiddo."

Georgie grinned super big, and I felt great. But there was one score left to settle.

"There's something Georgie left out," I said, staring right at Goon and holding up a purple marker. "Somebody used a purple marker to deface Georgie's campaign posters. So I asked Mr. Amato to do a chemical analysis of the ink in this marker and the ink that messed up the posters."

Goon got instantly incensed. "You went in my

room! Mom, I locked my room. How did he get in my room?" She glared at me. "Give me my marker."

"So you admit that this is your marker," I said. "And you admit that you drew mustaches on Georgie's posters."

"Not all of them!" she screamed. Then, realizing what she had said, she whined, "It was just a joke."

Mom sighed deeply. "We will discuss punishment after dinner, June. I am very disappointed."

Goon was majorly upset. And she should've been. We both know Mom is much tougher than Dad with punishments.

"But what about his trespassing?" Goon complained. "It's my room!"

I gave her a big grin. "I never went in your room. This *isn't* your marker. It's one exactly like it that I borrowed from Lana Shen today. And I never asked Mr. Amato to do anything."

Goon flung herself back in her chair and crossed her arms. She was steaming mad at how she'd given herself away. I did a quick Point Battle calculation. This one was big, and it could be even bigger!

Here's how I figured it. Goon had embarrassed herself. That was four points. Because I had tricked her into confessing in a very excellent way, it doubled to eight. She'd gotten punished by Mom. That was four more points. And since I was the one who turned her in, the whole thing was doubled to twenty-four points, making the score Goon: 694, Cheesie: 711!

And if Mom's punishment turned out to be really big, my points would double again to forty-eight, and I'd be ahead by forty-one points. Neither one of us had *ever* been that far ahead! And too bad the Point Battle didn't allow me to give myself points for doing a good deed by mailing the envelope.

Goon started stabbing her fork over and over into a potato on her plate, probably wishing it was me.

Sixth grade at RLS was turning out to be excellent.

Chapter 17

Zombies!

The next day, moments after I sat down in my homeroom, Mr. Stotts totally surprised me and everyone.

"And in the contest for sixth-grade president," he said over the loudspeaker, "something very unusual has happened."

I looked at Eddie. He seemed calm, but I didn't believe it. In the back row, Georgie was fidgeting, his eyebrows waggling up and down, a sure sign he was nervous.

"Of the two hundred fifty-three votes cast," Mr. Stotts announced, "Eddie Chapple received thirty-nine, Georgie Sinkoff forty-one, Diana Mooney forty-five, and, with a surprising one hundred twenty-eight write-in votes, the winner is Ronald Mack!"

"I thought I was the only one!" Georgie shouted. "I wrote your name in!"

"So did I," Lana said.

"Me too," Oddny said.

A bunch of other kids shouted they had, too.

"Congratulations," Eddie mumbled.

I must've been in a daze because the next thing I knew I was standing at Mrs. Wikowitz's desk.

"There must be some kind of mistake," I told her. "I need to talk to Mr. Stotts."

Moments later I was alone, walking toward the office. My mind was jumping from one thought to another.

This is crazy. . . .

Goon will go ballistic. . . .

Granpa will say he knew I was going to win. . . .

I was thinking so hard, I was unaware of anything outside my thoughts. The corridors were deserted. Classes were going on inside the rooms I passed, but I heard nothing. It was as if I were walking in a world of no sound.

Suddenly a huge raven swooped past me with a sharp caw, its wings almost touching my head. I jumped as the giant black bird turned and started back toward me. I grabbed the nearest doorknob—a janitor's closet—and yanked it open. I leaped inside and  pulled the door toward me, but the bird twisted sideways and flew in through the crack just before the door slammed shut.

It was pitch-dark. I could hear fluttering, and then nothing except the tremendously loud pounding of my own heart. I fumbled for the light switch.

The light clicked on. The raven was gone, transformed by some evil magic into a hideous, bloodthirsty zombie whose undead hands were reaching for my throat!

Chapter 18

The Curse of Diana

Fooled you!

Everything in the last chapter was fake. I just wanted to write about zombies.

And I didn't get a single write-in vote. It was actually Diana Mooney who won the election.

Georgie was depressed.

I was depressed.

And then it got worse.

Much worse.

Diana cornered me as I was walking to my math class. "You said for everyone to vote for the person who'd be the best sixth-grade president. Without your speech, I never would've won."

She was smiling and sort of rocking side to side with happiness. Lots of kids walked past us.

"Congratulations," I said without much enthusiasm.

She leaned close and spoke softly. "I owe you so much, Cheesie." Without warning, she gave me a huge hug and whispered, "Would you like to be my boyfriend?"

I squirgled (*squirmed* and *wiggled* REALLY HARD!) out of her grasp and ran.

I ran down the corridor.

I ran past the office.

I ran out of the school.

I ran like crazy!

I didn't stop running until I was eight blocks away.

Chapter 19

Georgie's Betrayal

Fooled you again!

Everything in the last chapter was also fake. The disappointing truth is that Eddie won the election. And that turned out to be the way worst thing that ever happened to me.

Here's why:

1. Over the next several weeks, Georgie started to act strangely.

2. He told me he thought he should've won the election and blamed me for losing.

3. I called him lots of times, but he always seemed busy.

4. He began going over to Eddie's house, and

pretty soon they were doing things that didn't include me.

Georgie and I had been best friends since we were two years old, and now, all because of a stupid election, the one friendship that meant everything to me was crumbling into a pile of dust.

It upset me so much, I can't even finish this chap . . .

Chapter 20

The Best Man Wins . . . Sort Of

If you believed *anything* in chapter 19, then I fooled you a third time! That whole chapter was maxitotally (*maximum* and *totally*) bogus!

Think about it. Georgie and I are BFF, and the last letter of that abbreviation stands for *FOREVER*.

The actual election results (and this is the real, absolute, honest truth) were:

Official 6th Grade Election results

Georgie Sinkoff	84	33.2%
Diana Mooney	82	32.4%
Eddie Chapple	82	32.4%
Santa Claus	5	2.0%
	253	100.0%

"It's a landslide!" Georgie screamed when he heard the news. "I totally crushed them!" Then he wiped his hand across his brow like he'd been sweating and whispered, "Whew."

Mrs. Wikowitz told us it was the closest election in the history of the sixth grade. And she should know. She's been at RLS since the school first opened.

Mr. Stotts called Georgie, Diana, and Eddie into his office to discuss the results. Georgie asked me to come along. Mr. Stotts didn't mind.

"Kids," he said, "to be declared the winner of most elections, you need a majority—you know, more than half—of the votes. Since none of you received a majority of the votes, we would normally set up a runoff election between the top two candidates. But since Diana and Eddie are tied, we'd have to flip a coin or leave all of you on the ballot. The first doesn't seem fair, and the second doesn't seem useful."

"You could just let Georgie win," Diana said. "He did get the most votes."

Georgie looked at the election tabulation on Mr.

Stotts's desk. "I don't think that's right. It was really close."

"If we have a runoff," Eddie said, "the jerks who wrote in Santa Claus shouldn't get to vote again."

Diana nodded in agreement.

There was a long pause. Then Georgie whispered in my ear, "This is sort of like what happened in the Cool Duel vote. You know . . . the tie."

(If you read my last book, you know what he was talking about. If you didn't . . . well, it would take too long to explain.)

Georgie smiled at me. It was a weird grin. Sometimes Georgie and I know exactly what the other is thinking. This was one of those times. I knew what he was going to say next.

"Mr. Stotts," Georgie announced, "I am officially canceling my vote for myself. I abstain."

Before anyone else could talk, I spoke up. "And so am I. That takes two votes off Georgie's total. Now it's a complete three-way tie."

Georgie pointed at Eddie and Diana. "And I say the three of us should be copresidents!"

Mr. Stotts looked at Diana . . . and then at Eddie . . . and then at Georgie. "That's a great idea," he said, a toothy smile lighting up his face.

He was right. It absolutely was one of Georgie's Great Ideas.

And that's how the election ended!

Chapter 21

The Finish Line

I am now finished with my third book. But I just had another adventure that included:

1. Giant earth-moving equipment
2. The sewer in front of my house
3. A pregnant cat
4. A very special gold ring . . . and
5. The mayor of Gloucester

So I've already started on my next book. There's lots of homework in middle school, but when I'm finished, the title will be on my website.

Goon got picked for the ballet thing in Boston, and I never did tell her I was the one who mailed her application. I am saving it in case I need it someday.

Mr. Sinkoff's and Ms. Dinnington's marriage plans got majorly messed up because of me and Georgie. (WHY and HOW are in my next book.)

Georgie is getting an A in science. He is also continuing to be very friendly with Oddny. I guess that's okay.

Mom punished Goon for the purple mustaches by grounding her for two weeks. No visiting any friends, and even worse, no cell phone when she's at home, which means no texting. Goon totally freaked, proving it was a REALLY BIG punishment, so I got another twenty-four points. I am hugely ahead: 735–694!

Bwa-ha-ha!

This chapter is called "The Finish Line" because I am really loving being on the XC team. Practice is hard but mucho rewarding. The races are fun. And the title of this book is totally true. I am running like crazy!

Thanks for reading all this. I really mean it. Because even if I don't know your name, I am your friend. (Maybe you could go to my website and say hi.)

Signed:

Ronald "Cheesie" Mack

Ronald "Cheesie" Mack (age 11 years and 3 months)

CheesieMack.com

The End

(There's actually more on the next page. It's about my website.)

Bonus Stuff

What You'll Find at CheesieMack.com

There's a bunch of new things from this book that are on my website (plus lots of stuff from my first two books):

1. Do you like this book or don't you or can't you make up your mind? (page 2)

2. The rules for the Point Battle. (page 5)

3. Excellent mulligans you've had. (page 40)

4. Mr. Amato's really cool experiments. (page 44)

5. Taste buds. (page 49)

6. Do you know any good fish jokes? (page 56)

7. Favorite-color survey. (page 73)

Acknowledgments

Cheesie couldn't have built his fabulous website without the Waxcreative Design team (waxcreative.com), led by Emily Cotler and Abi Bowling. Georgie wouldn't be such a good artist without the talents of cartoonist Violet Charles (bridgetovertroubledwaters.blogspot.com). And the plot wouldn't be as funny, clever, and tight without creative help from writers Julia Quinn (juliaquinn.com) and T. Zachary Cotler (winteranthology.com). *[Full disclosure: These are this author's five children.]*

Thanks also to editor Jim Thomas and agent Dan Lazar, whose understanding of the genre and the marketplace is wide, deep, and generously shared.

STEVE COTLER

is a retired Little League catcher who's also been a shoe salesman, telecom scientist, singer-songwriter, *Apollo 1* computer programmer, Hollywood screenwriter, Harvard Business School MBA, investment banker, and door-to-door egg man. He lives with his wife and writes in Sonoma County in Northern California's wine country. He thinks he is and always will be eleven years old.

DOUGLAS HOLGATE

is the illustrator of many notorious series for kids, including Super Chicken Nugget Boy, Planet Tad, Zack Proton, Zinc Alloy, and Bike Rider. Slowly but surely he is putting together a new, all-ages graphic novel, *Clementine Hetherington and the Button-Forbes Race*, co-created with critically acclaimed comics writer Jen Breach. If the Internet is on your computer, so is Douglas at www.skullduggery.com.au.

Visit Cheesie online at CheesieMack.com.
Visit Steve at SteveCotler.com.

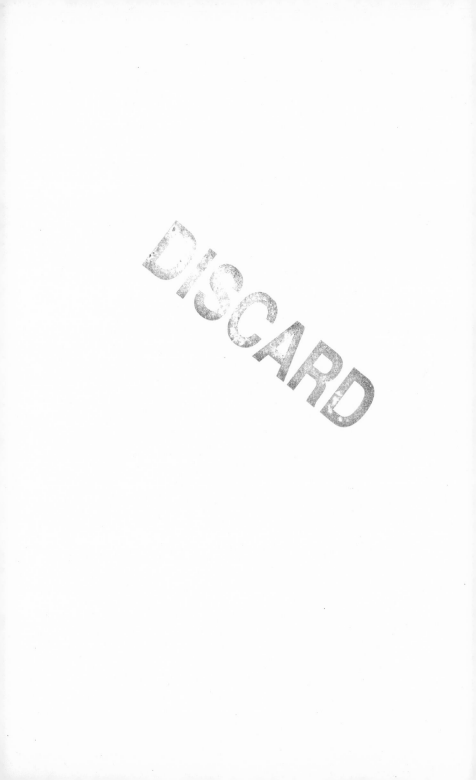